"Leon, is that why you made love to me?"

Merle took a deep shuddering breath. "I want to know if you made love to me so you could convince me to go with you to Calgary?"

"And why would I want to do that?" Leon asked warily.

"I can't scout your well if I'm in Calgary, can I?"

"Are you suggesting that I would prostitute myself to get you off this well?" His eyes were like hard jewels. "Perhaps I should be asking you the same question. Is that how you operate? I thought we had made love, but that wasn't what you were doing at all." Angry color was starting to build along his cheekbones. "What were you hoping for? That I would whisper pressure readings and core reports in your ear instead of endearments?"

She didn't care about the well anymore! She loved him, and she wanted him to love her, too. How could she have been so foolish?

SANDRA K. RHOADES began reading romance novels for relaxation when she was studying for her engineering degree and became completely hooked. She was amazed at how much fun the books are, and before long her sights were set on a career in romance writing. Colorado-born, she now lives in British Columbia with her husband and their two children. There she raises livestock, and every summer keeps a large garden.

SANDRA K. RHOADES

a risky business

Harlequin Books

TORONTO • NEW YORK • LONDON
AMSTERDAM • PARIS • SYDNEY • HAMBURG
STOCKHOLM • ATHENS • TOKYO • MILAN

Harlequin Presents first edition September 1986
ISBN 0-373-10917-2

Original hardcover edition published in 1986
by Mills & Boon Limited

CHAPTER ONE

MERLE'S hair was damp with perspiration beneath her battered Stetson. A trickle of sweat escaped the confines of the hat, trailing across her brow then down the bridge of her nose. Impatiently, she brushed it away and quickly returned her hand to the binoculars. She was lying prone, her elbows supporting part of her weight as she held the glasses steady. Finally, she saw the last section of drilling pipe emerge and the roughnecks move forward to remove the worn bit from the drill stem, their movements clumsy but co-ordinated as they negotiated the mud surrounding the hole.

Laying the glasses aside, she reached for her notebook and jotted down the number of sixty-foot drill pipe sections she had counted being taken from the well hole. Doing a quick multiplication in her head, she estimated the well depth then flipped through the pages of the book. The drillers appeared to have reached a hard layer, chert probably. She could have a few days off from watching the well now. They wouldn't be finding any petroleum in this layer.

Merle glanced up to take a final look at the well site and saw a figure emerge from the office trailer and move towards the rig. She identified the man as Greg Larson, the field geologist for the site. He was staying at the same motel as she was and she supposed she should spend the next few days getting closer to him.

At the thought, her mouth twisted into a grimace. She was already closer to Greg than she liked, but since she wanted to know the results of the exploratory well, the geologist was the logical one to tell her. At least Greg was too stupid to realise why she was dating him. Even so, keeping him happy, while at the same time stopping him from becoming too demanding emotionally and physically, wasn't the easiest task in the world.

Sighing, Merle gathered up her equipment and started placing it in the knapsack. She shouldn't let the thought of Greg's demands get to her. It was just part of the job. When you were scouting an oil well, you couldn't afford to leave any possible source of information untapped. The company drilling the well made it difficult enough to find out how things were going without letting yourself get squeamish about the methods you used.

Merle was almost ready to leave her position on the hilltop when she looked up and saw a black sports car pull up to the locked gate that was the only entrance to the drilling site. The security guard came out and after a brief conversation with the driver, unlocked the gate and motioned the car through. The car glided to a halt near the office and a man, dressed in a grey business suit and carrying a briefcase, slid out of the driver's side door.

Merle's curiosity was aroused. Obviously he was someone from the head office if the car and his mode of dress were anything to go by. Quickly, she retrieved her glasses from the knapsack and put them to her eyes. Very nice, she thought, moving the glasses to follow his progress as he walked towards the rig. Not movie-star handsome, but definitely attractive. His features were angular, with prominent cheekbones and a firm, square jaw line. His nose had a slight bump near the bridge, as though it had been broken at some time in the past. His complexion was deeply tanned, his light brown hair sunstreaked. If he was an oil executive, he either spent a lot of time in the field—or on holiday in the tropics.

When he reached Greg she studied the faces of the two men. Greg's face held that perpetually sullen air she knew only too well: even when he smiled, you never felt he was pleased with life. The other man's face had a certain charm; even though he wasn't smiling, he looked cheerful. Merle continued to stare at the man through the glasses. Perhaps cheerful wasn't the word; maybe content was more like it. Greg always had this underlying bitterness in him, as though he dwelled in life's little set-backs. This man appeared to be the sort who took what life threw at him and dealt with it, instead of brooding over it like Greg did.

She watched the two men talking together for several minutes longer, wishing she could read lips, before they turned to walk towards the office. Half-way across the yard the stranger halted, his eyes moving over the countryside surrounding the drilling site. Merle froze, holding her breath. Damn, she cursed silently. Had he seen something? A flash of light off the lens of the binoculars? Her heart was beating heavily in her chest and sweat collected across her brow. She didn't dare lower the glasses, afraid the movement might catch in the sunlight.

After an eternity, the man, shrugging slightly, motioned to the geologist and continued towards the office. It wasn't until she saw the door close behind them that Merle was able to unlock her frozen muscles and move. Hastily she repacked the knapsack and, moving in a crouch, left her position on the crest of the hill. Fortunately the earth was hard-packed and she would leave no betraying footsteps or depressions to indicate that someone had been using the hill as a vantage point to spy on the well site.

On the drive back to the motel Merle found herself thinking about the stranger at the well sote, weaving little fantasies about him. There had been something about him—an air of authority. I'll bet he likes having his own way, being the one in charge all the time, she thought. Maybe he wasn't that attractive after all. She didn't like men who tried to tell her what to do. Still, men that were too easily managed were boring after a while: he could be kind of a challenge.

God, Merle, you're getting weird, she derided herself as she turned into the motel parking lot. The chances of her ever seeing him again were remote. Very few oil executives made a habit of hanging around the rigs—they seemed to prefer the comfort of their offices.

She parked her Blazer and walked to her room, determinedly putting all thoughts of the man from the well site out of her mind. As she let herself into the room, the air pleasantly cooled by the air conditioner, she thanked God that at least this well was reasonably close to civilisation. While the motel wasn't exactly in the Hilton class, at least it was comfortable. On some jobs she had been forced to camp in the bush for weeks on end, driving out only to call in reports and restock her supplies.

Merle stripped off her dusty blue jeans and sweat-stained shirt, tossing them carelessly into the corner. Deciding to forgo a shower in favour of the swimming pool, she retrieved her white bikini from the floor of the bathroom where she had left it after her last swim, and headed for the pool. She swam for several minutes, then pulled herself out and lay face down on one of the padded loungers that edged the pool area. After unclasping the bra top of her bikini so her back wouldn't be marked, she gave herself up to the sensual pleasure of hot sun on bared flesh.

The steady hum of tyres on asphalt from the nearby highway combined with the heat created a soporific effect and Merle dozed. When she awoke it was to the sound of laughter and splashing from the pool. The sun had moved lower in the sky and the lounger where she lay was now in shade. She must have slept for hours. Awkwardly she reached back to do up the top of her bikini before rising.

'Allow me.' A deep, masculine voice threaded with amusement came from somewhere above her head and Merle froze. It's strange how, when startled, one's brain stops working, then, when it resumes functioning, the first thought is often totally irrelevant to the situation. In this instance, Merle's first thought was that the man had a British accent, a very *sexy* British accent.

She hadn't got far enough beyond this thought to react when she felt the edge of the lounger depress as someone sat down beside her. Strong hands removed the sections of the bikini from her lifeless fingers and deftly fastened the clasp. His fingers against her warm flesh raised the fine hairs along her spine, sending a shiver racing down her back as he let them linger. Merle remained motionless, her heart beating solidly in her chest. He momentarily caressed her rib cage, then left one hand resting lightly on the small of her back.

His hand seemed to burn through her skin, sending hot blood surging through her veins, and Merle jackknifed into a sitting position. She turned to face him, her cheeks flushed, her eyes flashing with outrage. 'Who . . .?' The question died in her throat. It was him, the man she had seen at the well site.

Close-up, he was better looking than she first thought, though still not handsome. His features were softened by the expression of amusement he wore, tiny lines of humour fanning out from the corners of his startling green eyes. His only covering was a pair of tightly fitting navy blue swimming briefs. He was deeply tanned, his chest covered by a mat of dark, curling hair. He looked very big, very sure of himself, and very male. Sexual awareness uncurled in the pit of her stomach and Merle swallowed hard, trying to suppress it. 'J-just what do you think you are doing?' she stammered.

He grinned broadly. 'I never could resist a lady in distress.' His eyes slid over her scantily clad form in intimate inspection. As his gaze rested on her breasts, partially revealed by the low cut of her bikini top, Merle's jaw tightened. *Don't tell me he's going to turn out to be a lecher.*

When he lifted his eyes to hers, a faint smile twitched on his lips as he read the outrage in her grey ones. 'You look hot and bothered,' he commented, laughing softly. 'Come for a swim with me.' He stood up and reached out to take her hand and pull her to her feet.

She didn't know if it was the impact of the physical awareness that he had on her, or the faint inflection of an order in his request, but whatever it was it reacted on her like a cattle prod. Merle flinched away from him, then in one quick movement rolled off the lounger on to her feet, putting it between them. She was a tall woman, but still she was forced to tip her head back to meet his eyes. In the corner of her vision she could see several people splashing about in the pool and was reassured by their presence. She tossed her head, the action disturbing the slick cap of her closely cropped black hair. With icy politeness, she said, 'If you'll excuse me.' She reached down and picked up her bottle of suntan oil, then moved to retrieve the hat that lay near the head of the lounger. The man seized it first and held it out to her, but when she went to take it from him, he snatched it back, grinning.

When he saw her expression, he again offered her the hat. 'I couldn't resist teasing you,' he explained, obviously puzzled by her cold glare. 'Let's start over. My name's Leon, what's yours?'

All else went out of her mind as Merle's brain went into overdrive. Leon—Leon Crane??? It had to be. Before scouting a well Merle made it a policy to find out something about the company who was doing the drilling. Puma Resources had been founded by Leon Crane, an Englishman who had arrived on the Calgary oil scene about three years ago. Prior to this, he had spent several years working in different countries around the world for various multi-national oil companies. Rumour had it that he came from a very wealthy, very prominent upper crust family whose backing had allowed him to start Puma Resources.

Not that he had needed the continued support of a wealthy family. During its first year of operation Puma had made a major find in the Peace River district, establishing it as one of the leaders among the hundreds of independent oil companies that abound in Alberta. That find had also established Leon Crane as a prominent figure in the oil world. He was frequently quoted in the financial pages and it was rumoured that the 'blue-eyed sheiks' of Alberta often sought his advice on energy policy.

As Merle studied him thoughtfully she remembered something else about Leon Crane. Not only was he featured in the business section of the newspapers, he was no stranger to the society pages, either. A bachelor, his name was frequently linked with that of some of the most beautiful women in Alberta society.

But whatever his social life was like, one fact remained: he would know all about what was happening at the well. She was suddenly swamped with indecision. Should she . . .? He was obviously attracted to her, she had seen that expression in enough men's eyes to know what it meant. She might never have another opportunity like this. He could be a heaven-sent source of information. Her eyes went to his, then skittered away uncertainly. She was having difficulty handling Greg but she had the feeling that that would be child's play compared to managing Leon Crane.

He was still watching her, one eyebrow lifted slightly as he waited for her to answer his question. She couldn't stand here dithering all day and only a fool would pass up a chance like this. Besides, hadn't she just told herself he would be a challenge? Her lips curved into a smile. 'Merle, my name's Merle Halliday.'

'Merle,' he said softly, testing the sound of it. 'I like that.'

He was still holding out the hat to her and now she accepted it, but didn't bother putting it on. She let her eyes hold his, injecting warm appreciation in them even though she knew she was playing a dangerous game. She would have to be very, very careful with this one. There was always a risk when you decided to use someone who attracted you; it wouldn't do to fall in love with them.

Their eyes held for several seconds, absorbed with one another, and neither of them was aware of the approaching footsteps. When a hard, male arm slipped around Merle's waist in a possessive gesture, she jumped. Her head swivelled in startled reaction and Greg pressed his mouth down hard on hers. The kiss ended almost before it began and as he released her, the geologist grinned down at her. 'Hi, honey. I see you've met my boss, Mr Crane.' He looked over to the other man, retaining his hold on her waist. 'Merle is staying here at the motel.'

'I see.' There was an odd note in his tone and Merle looked at him swiftly. His eyes were on Greg's arm where it rested about her waist, their expression veiled.

As if sensing the other man's interest, the geologist tightened his hold and Leon's mouth seemed to firm. Merle felt like screaming with frustration. Greg was going out of his way to make his claim on her apparent and there wasn't a thing she could do about it. She had been dating him for two weeks and if she gave him the cold shoulder now, he was bound to stage a scene.

Greg turned his attention back to Merle, a faint smile of satisfaction playing about his mouth. 'I came to tell you we would be leaving a little early for dinner tonight,' he said, dropping a kiss on her temple. 'I'm getting tired of the truckstop and thought it would be a nice change to drive into Medicine Hat for a meal.'

With difficulty, Merle bit back the urge to tell Greg exactly where she thought he should go for his evening meal. As if it wasn't enough that he was queering her pitch with Crane, did he have to *tell* her what they would be doing for dinner? Just because they usually ate together, didn't mean he could take it for granted that he could dictate her evening for her.

She glanced over to Leon. Why couldn't Greg have stayed away just a little longer? If she could have been sure of Crane, she would have dumped Greg. As it was, she didn't want to take the risk, so, since Greg was the bird in hand so to speak, she forced herself to smile at him. 'That sounds great. What time do you want to leave?'

He glanced at his watch. 'It's after five now. Can you be ready in an hour?'

Merle had started to agree when Leon Crane interposed, 'I'm sorry to disrupt your plans for the evening, but you and I have business to discuss.' He didn't look the least apologetic as his gaze rested on the other man. Since Greg had arrived on the scene Leon's potent charm seemed to have been placed into cold storage and Merle frowned slightly. He wasn't getting suspicious of her motive for dating Greg, was he? She shot both men a look from beneath her lashes. Greg was looking distinctly disgruntled, but she couldn't tell what Leon was thinking.

'I thought we had covered everything we needed to this afternoon,' the geologist protested.

'There are a few points that have occurred to me since then. I'd like to go over them tonight so I can head back to Calgary first thing in the morning. I'm sure Merle will understand.' His eyes flicked over her coldly and Merle felt a sense of relief. He was branding her a flirt, maybe even displaying a shade of sexual jealousy, but he didn't look suspicious.

Greg looked at her, his expression dismayed. 'Merle . . .?'

'Go ahead, Greg.' She didn't want Leon to get the idea she was possessive of Greg. Besides, it might undo a little of the damage Greg had done by his proprietary attitude if she let Leon know the change in plans didn't bother her. 'Business before pleasure, as they say. I could do with an early night anyway. I've a lot to do tomorrow.'

She disengaged Greg's arm from around her waist and started away.

'By the way, just what *do* you do?' Leon asked blandly before she had a chance to move more than a couple of paces away.

A jolt of shock shot through her and she hesitated a brief instant before turning back. She could only hope her face was convincingly innocent when she faced him. 'I'm a naturalist. I'm doing some research on the ecology of this area.'

'Research?' he asked, and Merle shot him a glance. His expression was only mildly curious and nothing else, so she forced herself to relax.

'That's right. I . . . I drive out into the countryside and study the life forms.' Why had she hesitated?

'It sounds very . . . interesting.' Why had *he* hesitated? 'Tell me, are you studying any particular life form?'

Merle wet her lips, her mouth dry. Her knowledge of biology was limited to the information gleaned from watching *The Nature of Things* on television and a few *Reader's Digest* articles. Generally she found that to be sufficient: most people were too interested in their own affairs to question her closely about her assumed occupation. 'Not any sp-specific one. I try to look at the situation as a whole. You know, the . . . uh . . . interaction of the different species.' She pulled the phrase out from her scanty memory file, shooting a surreptitious look at Crane. There was an odd light in those green eyes, almost as if he were amused by something—or dubious. She shivered slightly, and though it was from nerves she seized on it as an escape. 'It's getting cool out here. I think I'll go in now,' she said hastily. Without waiting for a reply from the other two, Merle turned quickly and left the pool area for her room.

CHAPTER TWO

THE next morning there was no sign of the black sports car in the motel parking lot when Merle went out to her Blazer to drive into Medicine Hat. She was still angry with herself for almost letting herself get tripped up by Leon Crane at the pool yesterday and had decided to go to the library and take out some books on ecology. She should have done that before ever starting the job. Even if she had to read every book they had on the subject, she was going to be prepared if anyone questioned her about her assumed occupation again.

It wouldn't hurt to call the company that had hired her, Wild Rose Petroleum, either, and see if one of their town scouts had heard anything about why Leon Crane had been out at the site. From what she had heard about him, it seemed odd that he should visit it personally.

Her visit to the library yielded several books on general biology and she also bought a field guide to Alberta wild flowers at the local bookstore. She could spend the next few days out on the prairie learning to identify the vegetation. If she were going to pretend she was an expert on life forms, she decided it would be easier to specialise in ones that wouldn't run away.

Before lunch, she found a phone booth and called Wild Rose. Though the Blazer was equipped with a mobile telephone, it was safer to use the pay phone. On a mobile phone, anyone else in the area who has one can overhear one side of the conversation.

Although it was unlikely that she would be able to conceal her identity as a scout indefinitely, the longer she could remain undercover the easier her job would be.

Her conversation with the contact at Wild Rose was brief. He had no better idea why Leon Crane had been out to the site than she did, but promised to see if he could find out something for her.

After hanging up the receiver, Merle stared at the phone for several seconds. She had lots of change in her purse, so there really wasn't a good excuse for not calling her mother. She would have to get it over with sometime, and as it was she had already delayed for two weeks. It wasn't going to be an easy conversation, though. Before she could talk herself out of calling, Merle picked up the receiver again and got the operator.

The phone at the other end of the line rang several times and Merle was just beginning to think she had been given a reprieve, when it was lifted off the hook. Quickly, Merle fed in the coins she had ready and greeted her mother.

'I was just thinking about you, Merle. I've tried calling you but there has been no answer at your apartment. I was on my way out, so we can't talk for long.'

'Okay, Mom, then I won't keep you. I just called to . . .'

'Wait a minute,' her mother interrupted. 'Why are you calling from a pay phone? Where are you?'

'Mom, I'm in Medicine Hat,' Merle answered quietly.

'Medicine Hat? Oh, Merle.' Why was it that you never got a poor connection when you really wanted one? Her mother's exasperation came over all too clearly on this line. 'I suppose you've given up your job with the construction company?'

'You knew it was only temporary, Mom . . . just something to tide me over until I got another scouting job.'

'That was a good job, Merle. I thought you liked it.'

'You know I hate that kind of work—stuck in some office building all day, typing and filing.'

Her mother sniffed audibly. 'If you had stayed with it, it would probably have got more interesting. It was the sort of job that could have led to . . .'

'Look, Mom,' Merle cut in, 'since you think it was so great, why don't you see if it's still open and you can take it? You'd love being surrounded by a bunch of gossipy women all day, hearing all about their love lives and their kids.'

'Sounds to me like you're jealous. You could get married and have children if you stopped running around the province playing spy.' Merle pressed her lips together tightly to avoid making a retort. She didn't want to get married—though try to convince her mother of that!

When her daughter remained silent, Mrs Halliday said, 'What about Jack? Is he willing to wait for you until you get back to Calgary? I'm sure he was serious about you.'

'Mother, I only went out with him a couple of times.' It had been an incredibly bad piece of luck that her mother had happened to be dining in the same restaurant on the night Merle had gone there with Jack Franklin. The next day she had been ready to order flowers for the wedding. That had been the last time Merle went out with Jack; she had been too embarrassed to accept another date. It was so humiliating to be out with someone who was little more than a casual acquaintance and have your mother show up and start vetting him as potential husband material.

'Well, I'm sure that something could have developed there if you had stayed in Calgary. He seemed like such a nice man; so attractive and with a good job, too. After all, darling, you are twenty-five. You'll be left on the shelf if you're not careful.'

'I happen to be quite happy "on the shelf" as you put it. Besides, you get married often enough for both of us.'

'Merle!' The hurt in her mother's voice came clearly over the phone line.

'I'm sorry, Mom,' Merle apologised hastily. 'That was a rotten thing to say.'

'Yes, it was. It is not my fault that your father died.'

Merle forestalled commenting on this remark to avoid further argument. As her mother said, it wasn't her fault that Merle's father had died when Merle was only a baby. However, she had been married twice since then in an attempt to replace him. Her excuse for the subsequent divorces was that no man was able to fill the shoes of her late first husband, though obviously she wasn't going to stop trying to find someone. Secretly, Merle felt that her parents' marriage would have ended in divorce as well, had Jake Halliday not died before her mother tired of him.

'Merle, I think you are very selfish. You know that I want grandchildren. Besides, I think you'd find that married life can be very satisfying. It's quite pleasant having a man look after you. You just haven't given it a chance.'

'We've had this argument before, Mom, so let's just drop it,' Merle said sharply. 'I only called to let you know where I am, in case you wanted to get in touch with me.' Merle went on to give her the name of the motel and its phone number. 'If I'm not there, you can try to get me on the mobile phone.'

Merle wondered that she didn't get frostbite from the icy silence that followed. Finally, she broke it, saying awkwardly, 'Well, then, if you're on your way out, I'll let you go.'

'Fine, though I doubt if I'll enjoy my lunch,' she grumbled. 'I'm having it with Marion Wells and you know what she's like. I told you her daughter just had another baby, didn't I? But then . . .'

Very gently, Merle replaced the receiver, cutting her mother off in mid-complaint. Just once she would like to talk to her mother without having to listen to her little speech on 'Why aren't you married and giving me grandchildren?' Not that Merle had any illusions as to why Edith Halliday (who always resumed her first husband's name following a divorce) was so keen to become a grandmother. She had reached the age when most of her friends' children had married and started families and she wanted to be able to compete with them. She wanted to be able to brag about the elegant church wedding she would stage, and show off the snapshots of her grandchildren.

And while she's passing around the photos, I'd be the one stuck at home changing nappies and catering to the whims of some man, Merle thought derisively. Only once, about five years ago, had she almost given in to her mother. At that time, she hadn't started her career as an oil scout and she had been working as a secretary for the same firm as Paul Garret. In the beginning, she had thought that she had finally met someone she could spend her life with. She was wearing his engagement ring before she discovered that with his plans for the future it would be more fitting to put it through her nose than on her finger.

Her mother had never quite forgiven her for breaking off with Paul, though Merle had never had any regrets. It wasn't until the break that Merle realised she had got involved with him more to please Edith than because she actually felt any deep emotion for him.

A dusty, red Puma Resources pick-up was in the parking lot when Merle returned from her trip to Medicine Hat. She recognised it as the one Greg usually drove and concluded that he had decided to take some time off while he had a chance. When the drillers reached a potential oil-bearing layer he would probably stay at the site twenty-four hours a day to analyse the rock samples coming up in drilling mud. Oil is found in layers of porous sedentary rock where it is trapped in the spaces between the rock particles. Greg's job would be to detect its presence by means of the various methods available to him, such as microscopic study of the rock samples, ultraviolet radiation, fluorescence, even odour and taste. Once having discovered petroleum, he would then conduct further tests to determine whether the oil and/or gas was present in commercial quantities. Only rarely was a reserve large enough and under sufficient pressure to produce the popular image of a 'gusher'.

After going to her room to change into her bikini, Merle left her room to go find Greg. She found him stretched out on one of the loungers next to the pool. As she walked towards him, she forced down a feeling of depression. His attitude towards her yesterday had irritated her. Greg Larson was just the sort of man that reinforced her determination to remain single. Merle could well imagine the kind of life he would offer any poor misguided woman who was fool enough to marry him. Not that he would object to his wife working. On the contrary, he would probably expect her to keep her job, as well as take care of all the housework, cooking, and laundry—and be grateful to him for his enlightened outlook towards a working wife.

Settling into the lounger next to him, Merle greeted Greg with a manufactured smile. He immediately started complaining about Leon Crane and his interference in their dinner plans last night. Though Merle knew she should be delighted with his attitude (there was no better source of information than a disgruntled employee with a slight persecution complex) coming on top of the phone conversation with her mother, Merle just wanted to turn him off like a boring television programme.

'He thinks he can throw his weight around because he's got a few bucks; can walk all over me because I'm only a poor working stiff.' Greg gestured with the cigarette in his hand, spilling ash on the concrete patio. Merle's eyes went to the grey flakes. Smoking at a drilling site was strictly forbidden and consequently, few oil men smoked. Those who used tobacco usually chewed snooze, a disgusting habit to Merle's mind. This was the first time Merle had seen Greg smoke. It had to be a gesture of defiance. No doubt about it, Greg was going to be a veritable gold mine of information. She turned her attention back to the conversation. 'But let me tell you this, Merle, I've got a contract with Puma and nothing in it says I have to let him tell me how to spend my free time,' Greg asserted hotly.

Suddenly he had all her attention. 'What do you mean?'

'Crane doesn't think I should be seeing you.'

She should have expected this, but none the less Greg's words jolted her. With studied casualness, Merle uncapped her suntan oil, and pouring a little into her palm, started spreading it over her legs. 'You must have misunderstood him,' she said, injecting her tone with innocent disbelief. 'What possible reason could he have for not wanting us to be friends?'

'It's this well I'm working on. It's supposed to be very hush-hush and he's afraid I might be indiscreet,' Greg explained.

'Indiscreet?' Merle looked up at him, feigning puzzlement. Warning bells were starting to ring in her head. Damn Leon Crane, why hadn't he just stayed in Calgary? She might not enjoy dating Greg, but he could save her hours of lying out in the hot sun. And now Leon was going to muzzle him ... damn, damn, *damn*.

'It's a test well and he thinks I might let slip some information about how it's going.'

Merle shrugged, slipping on her sunglasses to hide her eyes. To date, Greg had let slip very little on the well, but then, so far, there wasn't much he could tell her that would be interesting. However, it wasn't long before he *would* have valuable information on the status of the drilling and Merle knew she could extract it without his even realising it. Merle felt a surge of resentment against Crane. The carefully cultivated friendship she had established with Greg would be all for naught if he shut Greg up now.

Deciding that changing the subject at this point might appear suspicious, Merle decided on a role of well-feigned ignorance. 'A test well? What's that?'

'Our surface tests have indicated there might be petroleum in this area. We're drilling this well to find out if there is and how much,' Greg elaborated.

With an air of nonchalance, Merle said, 'So what? Why should I care if you find oil?'

'You might not be interested, but a lot of others would be,' he answered, a note of braggadocio entering his voice. 'The exploratory lease we got from the government only guarantees us half the rights to the development. The rest of the leases are up for grabs. If we find something, and can keep it secret until after the lease auction, we can tie up the whole field because the other guys won't know how to bid.' He looked over to her, obviously enjoying his role of teacher. 'Have you ever heard of an oil scout?'

Merle frowned and shook her head. This conversation would be quite amusing if she wasn't so worried about Greg clamming up on her.

'They're spies sent out by rival companies to find out about exploratory wells.'

She forced herself to laugh. 'And I suppose Mr Crane thinks I'm one of these spies. How melodramatic—and ridiculous.' With languid grace, she stretched supine on the lounger, aware that Greg was following her every movement. Merle had never had trouble attracting men. It was a useful asset in her job and she knew how to exploit it. At times she wondered what they saw in her, but as long as it worked she wasn't going to question it. Right now, she had better get Greg's mind off oil scouts before he started wondering about her.

Merle rolled on to her stomach and turned her head to smile at him. 'Would you mind oiling my back for me?'

'Of course not.' Greg eagerly scrambled up from his seat and picked up the bottle of suntan oil. As he smoothed the warm liquid over the skin of her back, Merle closed her eyes, revolted by her harlotry.

When his hands began to linger overlong, massaging the flesh on her midriff, Merle shifted uncomfortably and said, curtly, 'Thanks a lot, that should do it.' He removed his hands and she twisted her head to look at him. His face was flushed, a faint frown line forming between his brows. Greg was angered, and a little puzzled, by her continuing resistance to his advances. Merle wasn't too worried about it yet; she still had the upper hand in their relationship. None the less, she knew she would have to offer him some sop to his ego after rejecting him. 'Tell you what, I'll treat *you* to dinner tonight as a reward.'

'That would be great.' His face cleared and he beamed at her.

'Good,' Merle rested her head on her crossed arms and closed her eyes, smiling slightly. Leon Crane might want to gag Greg, but for the time being Merle was one step ahead of him—and she intended to keep it that way.

When Greg saw her at lunch five days later and told her that they wouldn't be able to see much of one another over the next few weeks due to job pressures, Merle wasn't surprised. She had been out to survey the well earlier that morning and could tell by the rate the 'kelly' was dropping that they were through the chert and into the softer, more porous rock below it.

The kelly was a long, square pipe located at the top of the drill stem where the drill mud was pumped in, and moved down slowly as the bit moved down. By timing the rate of descent, one could judge the type of rock the bit was moving through; the faster the kelly dropped, the softer the rock formation being encountered and the greater the likelihood of finding petroleum.

She had learned something else by watching the kelly. Although Leon Crane might have some suspicions about her, he didn't seem to be overly worried about someone watching the well. It wasn't uncommon for the driller to fake the dropping rate of the drill in an attempt to fool the scout watching the site. By slowing down the operation, he could try to make the scout think they were still in a non-oil-bearing formation and not in a potentially productive zone.

Later in the afternoon, Merle drove out to the site for another survey of the scene. As was her normal practice, she parked the Blazer a couple of miles away and walked the rest of the distance. Now that the drillers had reached a possible oil-bearing zone, she abandoned her surveillance post on the hilltop for a closer one. Although she could collect quite a bit of information through the binoculars, and even more using her spotting scope that magnified up to forty-five times, she wanted to be even closer now. Fortunately, there were several ravines running near the boundary fence and she could move quite close without being detected. Merle crept up one of them, carefully keeping out of sight and, crawling the last few yards, took up a position about thirty feet from the chain-link fence.

The first thing she noticed was Leon Crane's black sports car. What was the matter with the man? Didn't he *know* he was supposed to stay in his cushy office in Calgary and wait for the reports to come in instead of visiting the site? She quickly inspected the area around the rig and seeing neither Greg nor Crane, surmised that they must be working in the office. Just knowing Leon was nearby set her nerves on edge, though, and as there didn't seem to be much going on right now,

Merle beat a hasty retreat.

She took her time returning to the Blazer. Pulling out her wild flower guide, she decided to try matching the pictures in it to the vegetation around her. After a time, she found herself becoming engrossed in the exercise. By the time she neared her vehicle, Merle's arms wre filled with wild flowers. She had discovered some wild roses, Alberta's floral emblem, and when she got back to the motel, she would askt them at the desk if they had a vase she could borrow. Their bright pink petals would cheer up her room considerably.

She had almost reached her tan and white vehicle before she noticed the car parked behind it. Leon Crane was leaning negligently against the front of his black Ferrari, obviously waiting for her. Automatically she glanced over her shoulder, relieved to see that she had approached the truck from an entirely different direction than from where the well was sited. Nevertheless, her stomach ws knotted with tension when she walked over to greet him.

'Hi, I didn't expect to see you here.' She strove for a note of pleased surprise in her voice. The surprise was easy, but she had to work on the pleased part. For several seconds he remained silent, letting his gaze wander leisurely over her body. She grew acutely conscious of her dishevelled appearance under his perusal. Her clothes were none too clean after scrambling around in that gully and her skin felt caked with dust.

'I'm sure you didn't, Merle,' he said, his tone mocking. Althjough his expression was faintly amused, she sensed an underlying hostility. The knot in her stomach grew a little tighter. His eyes came to rest on the bundle of wild flowers in her arms. 'Collecting specimens?'

Merle's cheeks flushed as pink as the flowers she was carrying. She wasn't quite sure how a naturalist would handle the plants they collected, but she was pretty sure they didn't make them into bouquets. 'Not at all,' she answered airily. Until he actually accused her of scouting the well, she wasn't going to admit anything. 'I just picked these to put in my room at the motel.' She shifted the bouquet to one arm and dug in her pocket for the truck key. 'I'll put them in the cab.' She moved towards the passenger door of the Blazer.

'Here, let me help you,' he said suavely. Reaching out; he took her key before she realised his intention and proceeded to unlock the truck door.

As Merle carefully laid the flowers on the seat she was keenly aware of Leon Crane peering over her shoulder, inspecting the interior of the four-wheel drive. She heard his sudden intake of breath and knew he had spotted the mobile phone. It wasn't going to be easy to explain why she carried such an expensive piece of equipment. Thank God the spotting scope was tucked safely out of sight in her knapsack. If he saw *that* her goose would be cooked.

Assuming a casual air, Merle eased off her backpack and tossed it into the rear of the truck, wincing inwardly as it landed with a thud. The scope and binoculars represented an investment of several hundred dollars and she hoped they hadn't been damaged. But she didn't want Leon to become suspicious of what the pack might contain. He was watching her thoughtfully when she turned back to him, slamming the truck door as she did so. She forced herself to meet his eyes, opening hers wide in an innocent pose. 'Is something wrong?'

'I was just wondering why a biologist would need a mobile telephone.' His gaze never left her face.

Merle looked suitably blank for a moment, then let a smile take over. 'You noticed my phone? It's really something, isn't it? My mother got it for me when I graduated from university. She was concerned about my going out into a remote area and not being able to get in touch with anyone. You know how mothers are.' She laughed faintly, shrugging her shoulders with feigned casualness.

She felt the hard metal of the truck's door handle jabbing into her back and knew she had unconsciously backed away from him. The realisation only served to increase her nervousness and she found herself babbling on. 'Sh-she worries about me, being out here alone, I ... if the truck broke down ... er ... I wouldn't know how to fix it. I would be stranded ...' Her flow of words trickled to a halt. Leon remained silent, simply watching her and Merle dug her nails into her palms in an effort to get a grip on herself. She had no trouble lying to Greg, fabrications fell from her lips with the ease of water bubbling from an underground spring, but it wasn't that easy with his boss.

A faint breeze had sprung up and it ruffled the short strands of her dark hair. Leon's eyes seemed drawn by the movement and she smiled uncertainly at him. His gaze moved to her mouth, then lower, lingering on her breasts, their rise and fall erratic as tension affected her breathing. Was she imagining things or had he moved closer?

She wasn't imagining things. He leaned forward slightly and placed his hands against the truck cab on either side of her head, his arms forming a cage. Though he wasn't touching her, Merle felt almost as though he were. She could feel the heat of his body radiating across the inches that separated them. He smelled of perspiration, after-shave, and something else, something very male that sent her pulse galloping.

Merle knew he was watching her features, trying to read her thoughts. She kept her eyes trained on his throat, watching the steady throb of his pulse at its base. He should have been a basketball player, she thought distractedly. With most men she stood nearly at eye level, but to meet his eyes she would have to look up a long way. Dark hairs curled from the open neck of his shirt. She moistened her dry lips with her tongue, then swallowed hard. 'You . . .' she stopped to clear her throat but her voice remained husky, 'you were waiting for me. Did . . . did you have something you wanted to talk about?' She tipped her head up, forcing herself to look at his face.

His breath was warm and not unpleasant as it fanned her cheek. He was very close, she could see the pores of his skin, the faint stubble of whiskers that sprinkled his jaw. His eyes, dark unfathomable green, fastened on her mouth. Merle parted her lips in mute invitation.

He lowered his head and his mouth found hers, moving over it in erotic exploration. Initially her reaction was merely pretence, the surrender of her lips, the pressing of her body to his were the studied actions of an actress. She was in a tight spot, and if kissing her would divert his suspicions about her, then let him kiss her. But as his hands moved down her spine and his touch grew more demanding, she forgot she was playing a role. Conscious thought fled under the onslaught of the sensations he was awaking in her and instinct took over. The desire to acquiesce, to abandon herself to his touch overwhelmed saner impulses and she moulded her form to his.

Leon pulled her shirt free of her jeans and his fingers feathered along the bare flesh of her spine. Merle moaned softly as she felt herself being pulled into a vortex of passion, swept along by mindless desire. When his hand slipped down to her buttocks and forced her hips against his muscled thighs, she arched against him with wanton abandon.

He released her so suddenly she staggered back against the truck. For several seconds she stared at him in utter confusion, her mind fogged by the mists of passion. She felt bereft, a sailor stranded upon some foreign shore. Automatically, her hand went to her lips, gingerly touching them. They felt bruised and still tingled from the pressure of his lips.

Leon had moved a few feet away and was studying her with blatant interest. Nothing of what had just passed between them was reflected in his rugged features, but his eyes held a self-satisfied gleam. He made a slight movement in her direction and she recoiled.

'Now that we have that out of the way, let's have our little talk.'

His voice was so matter-of-fact Merle almost wondered if she had imagined that kiss. She stared blankly at him for a moment longer, then a black rage started to fill her. His kiss had been a calculated move to humiliate her! An icy calm descended over her, stiffening her spine. She had no trouble meeting his eyes as she leaned back against the Blazer, crossing her arms casually in front of her. 'What about?' she asked, her voice as crisp as a winter's day.

'Greg Larson—I want you to leave him alone.'

Merle arched her brows. So, that was what this was all about. 'I'm afraid I don't follow you. Just why should you be concerning yourself with our friend-ship?'

'Greg is my employee. Your "friendship", as you call it, is interfering with his ability to do his job. I want it stopped.' His features hardened with the order, his expression that of a man who expected to be obeyed.

Merle's grey eyes turned to hard chips of ice as they met his. 'And just how is it interfering? I only see Greg during his time off.'

'The next few weeks are critical to this job and I want Larson's full attention on it.'

He wouldn't make such an admission if he suspected her of scouting the well, and Merle suddenly wanted to laugh. Mr Leon Crane wasn't as clever as he thought he was! 'And you think my friendship with him diverts his attention? Oh, come on, Mr Crane,' she jeered, 'surely not even you are arrogant enough to believe you can dictate whom your employees may have as friends.'

His expression was glacial, his eyes dark with contempt. 'Obviously, I'm not making myself under-stood, so I'll put it in plain language. I don't like camp followers hanging around my men. I have enough problems with my workers out in the field without that. A man can't function when he spends all his time worrying about what his little bed-warmer is doing everytime his back is turned. So just lay off Larson—and any of the other men working for me you might decide to replace him with.'

White-hot fury flooded through her at his insult and she clenched her fist in order to control it. She felt like hitting him, smacking that arrogant look right off his face. 'You ... you insulting, sewer-minded ...' she sputtered. 'How dare you accuse me of such ...'

'Please, spare me the outrage,' Leon interposed in a faintly bored tone. 'I think I just had a pretty good demonstration of your 'virginal' reticence.'

A hard ball of rage seemed to block her throat, choking her, and her mouth opened and closed like a carp's. Granted, she wasn't a virgin, but she was a far cry from being what he was suggesting! Kissing a man didn't mean much, but going on from there was an entirely different story. The only man she had ever had that sort of relationship with was Paul, and then only after they had become engaged.

Leon started to laugh and he crossed the space that separated them in two strides. 'What's the matter, sweetheart? Disappointed because I didn't follow up on what you were offering?' His hand went to the nape of her neck, tangling in her hair and forcing her head back to look up at him. His voice dropped to a low, seductive pitch. 'Did you want us to lay out one of those sleeping bags you carry so conveniently in the back of your truck . . .?'

Merle tried to move away from him but his hold was such that the movement pulled her hair, bringing a muffled gasp of pain to her lips. 'Is that what you wanted, Merle? For me to take you right out here on the prairie?' he asked softly. In a quick movement, he grasped her wrists and forced them behind her back, where he shackled them in one hand. With firm, though not painful, pressure, he propelled her against him, forcing her body against his. With his other hand he tipped her face up to his.

Merle's breath came in slow, ragged gasps. His thighs were hard and intimate against hers, the warmth of his body soaking into her. Despite herself, her body was responding to him, her nipples hardening in arousal. Leon smiled as he noted them, clearly outlined through the thin cotton of her shirt. His thumb touched her lips, running seductively over her lower lip until they parted. 'Your invitation is coming in loud and clear, darling, but I'm afraid I'll have to decline.' His face expressed mocking regret. 'All I want from you is for you to leave Larson alone.' He released her and, turning on his heel, walked to his car. Merle heard the car door slam, then the powerful engine of the Ferrari flared to life. For several minutes, Merle could only stare blankly at the cloud of dust that lingered where it had been parked.

CHAPTER THREE

DAWN was breaking over the Alberta prairie when Merle drove into the motel parking lot. The indigo sky was gradually changing to turquoise and the cool morning air was filled with the concord of birds. Crossing the lot, Merle forced herself not to look in the direction of the black Ferrari. It was three days since her encounter with Leon and he still hadn't returned to Calgary. Fortunately, she had been able to avoid meeting him during that time, but it hadn't always been easy. There weren't that many restaurants to choose from in the area and twice she had revised her choice of eating establishment at the last minute upon discovering his car in the parking lot.

In her room Merle pulled off her soiled clothing, grimacing as she tossed them on to the pile of laundry that had collected in the corner. Somehow she would have to find the time to go into the nearest town and wash them today. The past few days had been hectic. Now that the drillers were into a potential oil-bearing zone, she was checking on the well every three to four hours. Generally she returned to the hotel so dusty and dirty she couldn't face wearing the same clothes again, and so the laundry pile had grown into a mountain.

After her shower Merle slipped into a silky nylon nightdress. It was a ridiculously feminine creation, pale peach trimmed with ivory lace insets over her bosom, but after scrambling around gullies half the night she felt the need for something to make her feel like a woman. It swirled around her bare feet as she walked over to the air conditioner and switched it on. It wasn't particularly warm in the room as yet, but the sound of the fan would mask the noise created when the other guests began stirring. Before sliding into bed she set her travel alarm for mid-morning.

Over an hour later she lay staring at the ceiling. Merle wasn't the type of person who normally dwelt on the unpleasant incidents that happened in life and the scene enacted out on the prairie with Crane the other afternoon certainly fell into that category! However, the whole, humiliating experience kept running through her mind. He had made a fool of her, kissing her like that, then labelling her a tramp. Just because she had responded to him didn't mean she slept with every man who made a pass at her—or that she would have slept with him either! And as for his accusations about her and Greg—.

Angrily, Merle turned over and thumped her pillow. Damn Leon Crane. She wasn't going to think about him anymore. Leaping out of the bed, she went into the bathroom and found the bottle of sleeping pills she kept for when her uncertain hours disrupted her sleep patterns. Taking out one of the small red capsules, she filled a glass with water and swallowed the pill. That was one way of getting the man out of her mind!

Merle arrived back at the motel around three in the afternoon. A cardboard box filled with clean laundry rested on the seat beside her and she planned to put it away before going out to the drilling rig. She was just inserting the room key in her door when she was hailed from behind.

She pushed her door open and turned around.

'Greg, what are you doing here? I thought you were working.' This was the first time she had seen him at the motel since her encounter with Leon.

He beamed at her. 'The rig broke down and they had to send for a new part. I figured I might as well take some time off while I had the chance.' He eyed the box she was still holding. 'Been doing laundry?'

Merle nodded. 'Yes, and this box weighs a ton. Come on in while I put it way.' She walked into the room and placed the box on the unmade bed.

'Gee, if I had known you were doing clothes today, I would have had you do mine, too,' Greg said, following her into the room.

Merle glanced at him quickly, sure that he couldn't be serious, but from his expression she saw that he was. 'Well . . . maybe next time,' she said awkwardly, turning her attention to the box of clothes. Do his laundry, indeed! That was just the sort of comment she would expect from him. The more she saw of Greg the less she liked him.

She had reached into the box and was lifting out a stack of folded denims, when she heard the door shut with a resounding click. Her heart lurched but she continued with her task, carrying the jeans over to the dresser and placing them in a drawer. When she turned to look at him again she noted a strange look of determination on his face.

What now? she thought, not liking the way his eyes had moved to the bed. Lately she had thought she had finally got it through to him what the limits to their physical relationship were. A few friendly kisses, but nothing more! Well, whatever he had in mind, he could forget it. Turning back to her laundry, she said, 'This won't take long. Why don't I meet you out by the pool when I've finished and we'll go for a swim?'

Greg came up behind her and slipped his arms around her. Lowering his head, he nuzzled her neck. 'Come on, Merle, you don't *really* want to go swimming, do you? Why don't you show me how much you've missed me?' His hands were making slow circles over her stomach. When he raised them to stroke her breasts, Merle jerked away.

She swung around to face him, her eyes flashing. 'I *said* I'd meet you by the pool later. Now, would you mind leaving my room so I can get on with my work?' She saw his mouth tighten and knew she should have controlled her temper. There must have been some tactful way of getting out of the situation without flying off the handle. She turned away from him, not wanting to look at him. 'I'm sorry, Greg. I shouldn't have snapped at you,' she offered conciliatorially.

'No, you shouldn't have,' he said, his voice hard. 'I've been looking forward to seeing you all week and this is the kind of welcome I get.'

'I know, I'm sorry.' Merle pushed her hair back form her forehead. 'It . . . it must be the heat. I guess it makes me grouchy.' She smiled at him tentatively. 'I really do need a swim, and afterwards . . . we never did have our dinner in Medicine Hat. Why don't we go tonight?'

He eyed her, the remnants of anger still evident in his face. After a moment he grudgingly agreed to her suggestion and left the room. When the door closed behind him, Merle sank down on to the edge of the bed and placed her head in her hands. He had left . . . but not until after he had kissed her. Nausea welled inside her and she jumped up and went into the bathroom. Taking up her toothbrush, she spread it with toothpaste then scrubbed her teeth until her gums were bleeding.

Going back into the bedroom, she wondered how she was going to make herself go out to the pool and see him. Leon was right about her. Oh, maybe she wasn't a camp follower, but she was little better than a common streetwalker. She was selling her body, using her sex to obtain information; not that she was sleeping with Greg, not that she would *ever* sleep with him. The idea gave her the shudders—just like the memory of his kiss did.

Suddenly she knew what she had to do. She couldn't stand it if he ever kissed her like that again. Gold mine or no gold mine, she was bailing out of this mess. She would go out to the pool right now and tell him she wasn't going out with him again. And if he caused a scene, well, he would just have to cause a scene. She had had enough.

Determined, Merle rushed to the door. She had it open before she stopped, then slowly closed it again, leaning dejectedly against it. 'Damn it,' she cursed softly. She couldn't just walk out there and baldly say, 'Sorry, Greg. You make me sick and I don't want to see you anymore.' He hadn't done anything she hadn't asked for. When he had kissed her so intimately she hadn't pushed him away but had stood passively in his arms.

Unhappily, Merle went back to her seat on the bed. She was still going to break it off, but she owed it to Greg to at least be tactful about it. She might not like him very much, but he didn't deserve to be callously hurt. Getting up again, Merle went to the bureau and rummaged in a drawer for a swimsuit. She would go swimming with him, then make some excuse for breaking their dinner date. Hopefully, he would be going back out to the rig tomorrow and she would have a few days' grace before he had any more time off. By then maybe she would have formulated some plan for letting him down easy.

A few minutes later Merle inspected her appearance in the mirror. The navy blue maillot she had chosen to wear was less revealing than the white bikini she usually wore, but it still looked better on her than she would have liked. Its dark colour made her hair look even blacker, bringing out the blue lights in it. Eyeing herself critically, she noticed she had lost a little weight since starting the job. With any luck, maybe she would lose some more and become so skinny Greg would lose interest without her having to reject him. On that thought, she picked up her towel and left her room.

To her relief there were a couple of children playing in the pool when she reached it. A young couple, probably their parents, were sitting on loungers watching them. At least she wouldn't have to go swimming with Greg alone. For a moment she thought she might even be able to avoid it altogether as she didn't see him anywhere. Then, at the far side of the pool, she noticed a lounger facing away from her with the shadow of a reclining man outlined beside it.

She might as well get it over with, she thought, and walked towards the figure. Years later she would still be able to recall the jolt she received when she reached the lounger and saw Leon Crane looking up at her with cool green eyes. More than once when she was out in the field, she had accidentally brushed against an electric fence, and the sensation that shot through her mid-section on seeing him was very similar.

Merle stood staring at him, unable to tear her eyes away from his or utter a word. Then, the whole humiliating scene played out on the prairie the other afternoon started running through her head and a slow blush inched up her cheeks.

'Hello, Merle.'

She swallowed with some difficulty. 'Hello.' Her voice came out as a whisper.

'Is something wrong? You seem surprised to see me.' His eyes crinkled at the corners.

Merle tore her eyes away from him, looking around somewhat wildly. 'Y-yes, I . . . uh . . . guess I am. I was expecting to see Greg.' She saw his eyebrows shoot up and added defiantly, 'We were going swimming.'

'Is that so?' Leon sat up and swung his legs over the edge of the lounger. It was a graceful movement for such a large man and Merle watched him dry-mouthed. His swimming trunks were very brief, stark white against the deep tan of his body. Compulsively, she stared at the ripple of muscles under bronzed skin as he flexed his shoulders slightly. He might not be the handsomest man she had ever seen, but there was a compelling attraction to him, an animal maleness that sent awareness snaking through her bloodstream.

'I meant what I said the other day, Merle. I don't want you hanging around Larson.' Though the words were spoken softly, there was an underlying firmness to them that warned her of his determination to be obeyed.

He stood suddenly, and involuntarily Merle took a step backwards. Her instinctive reaction to him annoyed her. She was not by nature timid, and that Leon had the power to disconcert her so easily sent anger surging through her. She would *not* let him intimidate her! He had already made a fool of her once and she wasn't going to let him do it again.

Her head tilted at a defiant angle, the muscles of her jaw tightening with determination. 'I'm sorry to disappoint you, but I please myself. If I want to see Greg Larson, then that is exactly what I will do.'

He came to stand directly in front of her, and she forced herself to stand her ground. 'You think so?' he asked silkily. His hand reached up and traced an imaginary line from her ear lobe, down her throat to the swell of her bosom before dropping to his side again. 'You're not seeing him now. He went back to work.'

Her tongue slipped out to wet her lips. She found it difficult to breathe let alone think when he was standing so close to her. His touch had sent her thoughts into total chaos.

At her prolonged silence, he continued softly, 'I'm sure I can entertain you just as well as he can. Why don't we have dinner together and I'll show you?' He lifted her wrist and his thumb caressed her pulse seductively, then he lowered his head to brush her palm with his lips.

When he looked back at her, Merle stared up into his eyes for several seconds. Though she knew she shouldn't even consider going with him, she felt herself wavering. Going out with his boss would help her get rid of Greg. And in terms of usefulness, Leon would know just as much as Greg about the well, even more. On the other hand, Leon was obviously a lot smarter than Greg so it wouldn't be nearly as easy to mine him for information.

Her indecision must have been reflected in her features, because he suddenly said, 'Would it help you make your decision if I said I was sorry for saying those things to you the other afternoon?'

She searched his face, her brow pleated with puzzlement. The last thing she had expected from him was an apology. Had he changed his opinion of her? If he had, then why was he still insisting she stop seeing Greg? Was it because he had figured out the truth? Her face paled slightly at that thought. On the other hand, why would he want to go out with her if that was the case?

'I'd like to have dinner with you,' Merle finally said. The only way of finding out would be to go with him. If he had found out she was scouting the well, she had to know. He couldn't stop her, but it meant the drillers could start throwing some red herrings in her direction and she would have to be alert for them.

'Good. I suggest we drive into Medicine Hat for it,' he said, smiling down at her. Merle thought she detected a trace of triumph in his expression but when he glanced back at her after checking his watch, she decided she had imagined it. 'I have some business to attend to this afternoon, so I'll pick you up around six-thirty.'

'Fine,' she hesitated, then, 'why don't we meet in the parking lot?' He gave her a curious look, but nodded his agreement. She didn't want him to see her room. It wasn't that she had anything lying around that suggested she was scouting the well. What notes she kept in the room were carefully wrapped in the spare blanket on the wardrobe shelf, but nevertheless she was reluctant for him to get even that close to them. Besides, she had never finished putting her laundry away and the place was a mess.

'I'll see you then.' With a slight wave of his hand he walked away, leaving the pool area.

Merle had just decided she might as well go ahead with her swim, when she remembered the other part of his remarks. Business—she should go out to the site to see what was going on. She glanced up at the cloudless blue sky, the burning orb of the sun, then looked longingly at the pool. It was mid-afternoon and the temperature was in the nineties. It would take her at least two hours to check the site, longer if she had to spend much time watching it.

On the other hand, she could just drive by it. She would be able to tell if they were still shut down, and if that was where Leon had gone. But Leon did know she drove the Blazer and if he noticed her driving past he was sure to mention it.

'Oh, the heck with it,' she muttered, going to the edge of the pool and diving in. She could always go out after she got back from her date with Leon. If it looked like she might have missed something, she would pump Greg about it the next time she saw him.

She spent the rest of the afternoon in the pool trying to keep cool, then left it to get ready for her date. It didn't take long. After all, it wasn't as if she had to spend hours deciding on what to wear. She had only two dresses with her, having left the bulk of her wardrobe at her apartment in Calgary. The one she chose to wear, an apricot shift with a halter top that left her back bared to the waist, was definitely the dressier of the two. It was made from pure silk and cut with the flare that only a top designer could achieve. The warm colour accentuated her tan and, with her dark hair, gave her an exotic look that spelled 'class'. It had been wickedly expensive, Merle recalled, her eyes sparkling with remembered extravagance.

She picked up the flagon of Joy perfume and shook out a few drops to dab on her pulse points. Holding it to the light, she saw the bottle was nearly empty. As soon as she got her next paycheque she would have to replace it. Her mother was always on to her to open a savings account, but to Merle's mind there wasn't much point in working if you didn't treat yourself to a few luxuries now and then.

When she reached the parking lot a few minutes later, she didn't see Leon immediately, though the Ferrari was parked near her Blazer. Glancing at her watch, she saw she was five minutes early, and wondered whether she should go back to her room and wait a few minutes. Being unpaved, the parking lot was dusty, especially at this time of day when the tourists were starting to pull in for the night.

She had just decided to go back inside, when she saw Leon come around the rear of the Blazer. That he had been examining the vehicle, peering into the windows, was obvious. Leon saw her and, when he motioned her to join him, she had little recourse but to walk over to him. Her heart was beating rapidly when she reached him, but she managed to keep her consternation out of her expression as she returned his smile.

'I was just having a look at your truck,' Leon commented, turning his head away to peer into the rear window.

'Oh.' It took a lot of effort to get even that single syllable out.

'It has a lot of cargo space with the rear seat removed like that. I need a different vehicle,' he explained. 'The Ferrari is great for the city and the highway, but the dirt roads around here are pretty hard on it. I was going to use one of the company pick-ups but I like the look of this. How do you find it?' He turned back to her.

'I really like it.' Her relief was reflected in the brilliance of the smile she gave him. 'The four-wheel drive is handy and like you say, you can carry a lot of equipment in it.'

'Yes,' he nodded thoughtfully, eyeing the camping equipment in the rear of the truck. 'I certainly couldn't get that lot in the boot of the Ferrari.'

'Boot?' Merle frowned, then laughed. 'Oh, you mean the trunk. Sometimes I forget you come from England.'

'You mean I'm losing my accent?' One eyebrow lifted in amused enquiry.

She shook her head, laughing. 'Not when you say something odd like boot.'

'Odd?' His tone was affronted but his eyes held a mischievous sparkle. 'I'll have you know, I speak the Queen's English. I can't imagine why you colonials refuse to learn the proper names for things,' he said haughtily, peering down his nose at her.

'I'm terribly sorry, sir,' Merle affected a curtsey, attempting to copy his accent. 'In future I shall only call it a boot and the hood will become the bonnet. Now, what should I call the jockey box?'

She started to giggle when she saw she had him stumped. After a moment, he joined in, then asked, 'Okay, I give in. What in heaven's name is a jockey box?'

Merle pursed her lips, her eyes twinkling. 'You don't know? I don't think that I should tell you. After all, if you haven't bothered to learn the proper names for things . . .?' She shrugged, helplessly.

'Merle,' he warned sternly, stepping towards her. He grasped her shoulders in a gentle hold. 'I have vays of making you talk.'

'Your German accent is terrible,' Merle laughed up at him. 'Not the least threatening.'

'It can't be worse than your attempt at what I assume was an English accent,' he retaliated, smiling down at her. Their eyes held for several seconds, and the amusement left her face. *Damn, he was attractive.* His hands were warm against her bared shoulders and awareness rippled down her spine. Her heart thumped heavily in her breast as she saw the smile fade from his lips and his eyes darken. He felt it, too: the electric tension that had sprung up between them.

A car horn blared behind them, startling them back to awareness of their surroundings. 'Hey, buddy, you're blocking the drive!' The driver of the car had rolled down his window to shout at them. 'Get her to the room before you start fooling around.'

Leon shot the man a hard look, then taking Merle's elbow led her to the Ferrari. Her cheeks were flushed, her face averted as he helped her into the passenger seat. It was foolish to let the man's crude remark embarrass her. After all, they hadn't been doing anything. Leon hadn't even been embracing her, let alone kissing her. They had only been looking at each other.

Part of her embarrassment was that it had reminded her of Leon's opinion of her. She still didn't know whether he had changed it or not. Was he thinking she was the sort of woman who went to motel rooms with men? She shot him a quick glance. His head was turned away from her as he checked for oncoming traffic before entering the highway. When he turned back, Merle quickly looked out the side window.

They rode in silence and after a few minutes, Merle felt some of the tension drain away from her. If he wasn't going to comment on the man in the parking lot, she certainly wasn't going to bring him up.

The car was extremely comfortable, the fine leather upholstery and plush carpeting luxurious after the practicality of the Blazer. She certainly hoped that Leon's only interest in the Blazer was because he was thinking of getting one. It wouldn't be a major disaster if he learned her true purpose for being in the area, but she still didn't want him to know. Sliding him another glance, she admitted it wasn't only that remaining undercover made her job easier. She was attracted to Leon and even if nothing could come of it, she didn't want him to know she was working against him.

They had gone several miles before Leon broke the silence. 'You never did tell me.'

'Tell you?' Merle pulled her eyes away from the pasing scenery to look at him.

'What a jockey box is?'

'Oh, it's the glove compartment.'

'You mean the glove box,' he corrected, smiling across at her. Though she returned his smile, somehow their earlier comraderie had vanished, the joke gone flat. Merle settled back against her seat again, aware that the ensuing silence was faintly oppressive.

A few more minutes passed, then Leon said, 'You're very quiet. What are you thinking?'

Merle turned to look at him. What would he say if she told him she was wondering why he had asked her out? Had he invited her because he had changed his mind about her ... or because he hadn't? Was he planning to take up where he had left off the other afternoon? But, she couldn't voice those questions, so instead she said, 'Actually, I was thinking I'd take a day off and drive up to the Badlands while I'm in the area.'

'Have you been there before?'

'Several times, I find it a fascinating area. All the hoodoos and pinnacles give it such an out of this world atmosphere.'

'Yes,' Leon agreed, 'it's amazing what wind and water can do, creating sculptures that rival some of the great art works of man. In some places around there, erosion has exposed strata that was laid down seventy million years ago. What area were you thinking of going to?'

'I thought I'd go up to Dinosaur Provincial Park. The views are spectacular in that area as it's about eight miles from rimrock to rimrock. I always like to visit the museum displays, too. Buildings are erected right where the dinosaur skeletons were uncovered in the rock. It's kind of fantastic when you realise you're looking at the remains of something that lived over sixty-five millions years ago.'

For a few minutes they discussed the attractions of the park, which Leon had also visited, then he asked, 'Are you going to see if you can find some dinosaur bones on your own?'

'Of course,' Merle grinned at him. 'That's one of the draws of the area. There are fossils lying all over the place, not just from dinosaurs.' Collecting fossils was one of her favourite hobbies and when Leon admitted he also had a collection, the conversation flowed smoothly for the remainder of the drive into Medicine Hat as they compared notes.

It wasn't until they were seated in the dimly-lit restaurant Leon had chosen for their meal, that Merle realised she might have been indiscreet. Her interest in paleontology could seem strange when she was supposedly a biologist. Not that she thought about it, Leon had cast her several odd looks during their talk but she hadn't paid any attention to them. Fossils weren't exactly everyone's favourite topic of conversation and she had let her enthusiasm at finding someone who shared her interest override her prudence.

Her nervousness increased when she glanced up to see Leon eyeing her speculatively. Someone should cut her tongue out. If he was suspecting her now, it was her own fault. Her spirits plunged even further when he suddenly frowned heavily and said, 'You surprise me, Merle. You're obviously very intelligent. I don't understand how you could have been so foolish as to start an affair with Larson.'

Merle took a large swallow from the cocktail she had ordered earlier. She knew that she should be relieved that he hadn't figured out she was scouting the well, but still she was disappointed that he hadn't changed his mind about her. Keeping her eyes trained on the drink sitting in front of her, she chewed her lower lip. She wanted to defend herself, explain that he was wrong about her relationship with Greg, but she realised she would have to remain silent. Not only would it undoubtedly be pointless, but dangerous as well. As long as he thought she was involved in a passionate love affair with Greg, he wouldn't suspect her real reason for seeing the geologist.

Having reached this conclusion, she was totally unprepared for his next words. 'You should have realised that as soon as the rumour of your "friendship" reached head office, I would check you out.'

CHAPTER FOUR

MERLE looked up at him quickly. His expression was amused, as though he were enjoying the confused mingling of emotions that played across her features. And he wasn't angry—did that mean he hadn't found out? But if he had checked her out, he had to know. And if he knew, he would be angry. Merle had a very logical mind. Given a set of facts, with computer-like efficiency she arrived at a conclusion. Unfortunately, with these facts she was caught in an illogical loop that seemed to have no exit.

'Is something wrong, Merle?' Leon asked mildly.

'Wrong?' she asked hoarsely.

'You seem a little . . . disconcerted?'

Her lips drew into a narrow line at the mocking question. Leon Crane was enjoying himself immensely at her expense! 'Should I be?' she asked curtly, her chest tightening with impotent anger.

He laughed softly. 'Why, not at all. You didn't really think I wouldn't see through your little act, did you? A naturalist studying, what was it, the interaction of the different species. Really, I'm ashamed of you. You could have come up with a better cover than that.'

The waiter arrived with their first course, which should have given Merle a chance to bring her anger and embarrassment under control but didn't. She speared a piece of crab viciously with her seafood fork, imagining it was Leon Crane she was stabbing. She would rather he had been angry than this . . . this laughing at her. He was treating her like an imcompetent ninny, and was obviously not the least bit worried about her scouting his well.

'These prawns are delicious. How's the crab?' Leon asked pleasantly when Merle had remained silently fuming for several minutes.

'Fine.' She didn't look up; the word was forced through clenched teeth.

'Are you going to pout all evening, Merle? After all, you're the one scouting my well, not the other way around,' he said reasonably.

'I'm not pouting,' Merle said mutinously, then after a silence asked, 'how long have you known?'

'That you were spying on the site? I suspected you as soon as I saw you with Larson and it didn't take long to have my suspicions confirmed.'

She raised her head to look at him, her forehead faintly creased. 'Then why . . .?'

'Haven't I said anything sooner?' he completed the question for her. 'Several reasons; for one thing, I was hoping to get Larson to come to his senses. Actually, I thought that maybe he had until I saw you at the pool this afternoon. You really have him wrapped around your little finger, don't you? Too bad it's cost him his job.' He took another bite of his seafood, chewing slowly as he savoured the delicate flavour of the prawns.

'You fired him?'

'I wasn't given much choice. I told him you were scouting the well and to stay away from you, but he didn't want to listen.' He shrugged slightly, as if firing his field geologist was as inconsequential as crushing a fly. He looked up from his plate and smiled across at her. Seeing her expression, he commented, 'You look puzzled, Merle.'

She was. Finally, she pushed away her half-eaten starter and frowned at him. 'You're awfully calm about the whole thing.'

'You expected me to be angry?'

'Naturally.'

'I was, at first,' he admitted. 'That's one of the reasons I was so hard on you the other afternoon. That, and I wanted to teach you a lesson. But it would be rather stupid to stay angry. This is the oil business and as long as the leasing system remains as it is, scouts are going to be part of it. Puma uses scouts, so I can hardly complain when other companies do the same.'

Their salads arrived, along with the bottle of white wine Leon had ordered. Through lowered lashes, Merle watched as Leon attended to the ritual sampling of the wine, admitting to a grudging admiration for him. His was the only sensible attitude to take, but she knew if their positions had been reversed she would never be so reasonable.

When the waiter left, Leon tasted his salad, then looked across at her. 'Don't misunderstand my attitude, Merle. Just because I understand about your scouting my well, that doesn't mean I'll help you do your job,' he warned. 'In fact, I'll be doing everything possible to make it more difficult for you.' He hesitated a moment, then added, 'And don't waste your time trying your Mata Hari tricks on me.'

'Is that what you meant when you said you wanted to teach me a lesson the other afternoon?' Merle didn't enjoy bringing that humiliating experience into the conversation, but she wanted to know.

'That was part of the lesson. I wanted you to understand that while I might enjoy making love to you, you're not going to seduce any information out of me. I also thought it was important for you to realise just what sort of dangerous game you were playing.'

Merle's eyes were puzzled as she looked over to him. 'I don't understand.'

'Then it's about time you did. I think I have a pretty good idea of what your relationship with Larson was. You were stringing him along with a lot of empty promises, weren't you? In less polite terms, you were being a tease.' He eyed her sternly. 'Am I right, Merle?'

She was forced to nod, her cheeks starting to burn. It was a relief to know he had revised his opinion of her but also embarrassing. However, she still didn't understand what he was getting at, and finally told him so.

'I don't want you turning your attention to another one of my workers now that I've got rid of Larson. That would be trouble, Merle.' There was no mocking amusement in his face now. Leon was deadly serious. 'Larson's told the rig workers he had a far more intimate relationship with you. They figure you've been putting out for him and if you start up with one of them now, he isn't going to let you keep things platonic. He'll want what he figures Larson got.'

She remembered what he had said about making her job more difficult and interrupted him impatiently, 'How do I know you're not telling me this just so I won't try to develop another contact?'

'The other afternoon I think I showed you just how vulnerable you are. If I had wanted you, you couldn't have stopped me,' he said harshly.

'If I had wanted you.' For some reason the words stung and Merle retorted, 'Oh, really? I know how to take care of myself, Mr Crane.'

'Stop being ridiculous, Merle. You may be able to

handle what a lot of people would consider a man's job, but you are *not* a man. You're smaller and you're weaker. I don't want one of my workers sent up on a rape charge, and I don't think you want that, either.'

Merle swallowed hard, taking sudden interest in the play of the candlelight on her wine glass. The cold truth of his words rang through her head. She liked to think of herself as independent, capable, in complete control of her life. Vulnerable—it wasn't an adjective she cared to use in connection with herself. It smacked of helplessness, dependence, submission. She didn't want to be any of those things.

The waiter brought their entrées, eyeing them curiously as he set the plates in front of them. When he had gone Merle picked up her fork, though in all truth she had little desire for food. She sensed Leon watching her, his own plate ignored, but she didn't want to meet his gaze. Although her anger had for the most part dissolved, she felt a lingering resentment against him. She was aware that there were perils in her occupation and guarded against them. She didn't like snakes, so she kept a sharp eye out for them. When working in the northern bush, she was careful with litter so as not to attract bears. She was cautious, but did not like admitting she was sometimes afraid of the hazards she encountered. But with Leon's talk of vulnerability, of weakness, an element of trepidation had crept into her inviolable self-confidence.

'Merle,' Leon spoke softly, taking her hand in his. 'You know I'm right, even if you don't want to admit it. I want you to promise me you won't do anything foolish.'

He squeezed her fingers lightly, and Merle found his eyes with hers. His were soft green and somehow tender as they met hers. Somewhat to her astonishment, she found herself making the promise. She had the strangest feeling that his eyes were telling her that he would make sure that nothing would happen to her. It was perhaps even stranger that she was comforted by the thought. She had never desired a man's protection, had never wanted to feel reliant on a man, yet she wanted to think that Leon would be looking out for her.

It was after midnight by the time they returned to the motel. After obtaining Merle's promise, Leon had turned out to be a most enjoyable dinner companion. In addition to their mutual interest in fossils and geology, they discovered they shared similar tastes in music and literature. Occasionally, they had disagreed, but their clashes were on the order of lively discussions rather than arguments. When the conversation had centred on geology, Merle hadn't been able to resist venturing a leading question, though Leon's chastening look and deft change of the subject convinced her she was wasting her time.

These thoughts occupied her as she got ready for bed, but once beneath the sheets, the lights off and her alarm set for dawn, Merle found sleep elusive. All evening she had been aware of the current of sexual tension flowing between them. Though he had treated her with friendly impersonality throughout the evening, on occasion she had looked up from her meal to find him watching her, the expression in his eyes telling her that he was aware of the chemistry between them.

She shifted in her bed, impatient with the restlessness that kept her awake. He hadn't even kissed her good night, for crying out loud! But before . . . he had kissed her before, a little voice in her head whispered. She placed her fingertips to her lips, remembering his touch. Her mind wandered to that afternoon out on the prairie, the memory of his body pressed against hers, the sensuous movement of his mouth over hers. Leon Crane would be an expert lover, passionate, demanding, capable of bringing a woman to the heights with him.

'Oh . . . shut up!' Merle admonished the persistent voice. Turning over, she pulled the pillow over her head.

When Merle awoke the next morning she felt rested and strangely happy. Her natural self-confidence had reasserted itself during sleep and in the morning light Leon's warning about staying away from the rig workers seemed misplaced. Though she was still feeling very warmly disposed towards him and was sure he was sincere in his concern about what might happen if she ignored his advice, she felt he was being overly apprehensive.

Not that she intended breaking her promise. It would be a waste of time. Even if she did manage to start a friendship with one of the workers, after Leon's dismissal of Greg, she was sure the man would be fired before he could be of any value to her. Nonetheless, her conviction that she could handle his employees restored her sense of well-being.

Over the next two days she didn't see Leon at either the motel or the well site and concluded he must have returned to Calgary the morning following their night out—probably to arrange for a new field geologist. Greg Larson was conspicuous by his absence, and Merle finally questioned the motel manageress about him. Apparently he had checked out the evening Leon had taken her out to dinner. She couldn't help wondering if Leon had taken her to Medicine Hat to keep her out of the way while Greg was making his departure.

But even though she didn't see him, Leon Crane was very much in her thoughts. Though she was still impressed by his lack of animosity towards her, it was tempting to interpret his very reasonableness as a sign of weakness—a weakness she could perhaps exploit? If he had been angry, she knew she would have had no chance in developing a friendship with him—but he hadn't been angry. Granted he was very shrewd, but he was also attracted to her. Long ago, Merle had decided that men were ruled by their hormones and not their heads. While in pursuit of a female of the species, they tended to forget everything else, including prudence. She wouldn't even need to feel guilty about extracting information from him. After all, he knew who she was, so it she happened to out-wit him, it would be perfectly fair.

Her conviction that she could manipulate Leon for her own purposes increased over the next couple of days. He had stated he would make her job even more difficult, but now that she was no longer working undercover she discovered it was, in fact, even easier. She no longer had to be as careful to conceal her surveillance activities since the rig workers knew they were being scouted. Consequently, she could park the Blazer closer to the site, and move right up to the fence whenever she wanted to observe the drilling. Unfortunately, the rig was shut down during these two days, waiting for a part for the piece of equipment that had broken to arrive, but Merle could envision her job being considerably easier once the drilling resumed.

Thus, Merle almost laughed with anticipation when she drove by the well site on the third morning and saw that the rig was once again in operation. This job was going to be a piece of cake! She parked the Blazer at the side of the road a mere half-mile from the site fence and jumped out. Shouldering her knapsack, she crossed a short stretch of prairie, then crawled through a four-strand barbed wire boundary fence several hundred yards from the chain-link perimeter fencing surrounding the site.

The terrain bordering the well was rough and uneven so Merle kept her eyes on the ground as she negotiated the gullies and hillocks. She was just scrambling out of a shallow ravine, when a harsh voice startled her. 'Just hold it right there, lady!'

Merle's head flew up to find a man, accompanied by a large, black dog, standing in her path. The man, of indeterminate age, was dressed in worn, faded blue overalls and a checked flannel workshirt. A battered, sweat-stained cowboy hat shaded a rugged, deeply tanned face set with hard, brown eyes. Before Merle could gather her scattered wits, he continued, 'This land's posted. You just better head back the way you came.'

'Posted?' Merle echoed, then recalled the tattered no-trespassing sign on one of the fence posts behind her. It had been there since she started scouting the site and until now, she had ignored it. No one had approached her before, so it hadn't seemed to have any significance. After all, she wasn't doing any damage to the property, as she quickly assured the rancher.

'I don't care what you're doing,' the man stated flatly. 'This is my land and you're trespassing on it. I want you off.'

'But . . .'

'You don't want me to have old Laddie Boy here help you, do you?' he interrupted. For the first time,

Merle took a good look at the dog. It was a large animal, standing thigh-high to the man. He looked like some sort of Shepherd-cross, with bristly, black hair that appeared to have never seen a grooming brush. The dog was staring at her with small, mean-looking black eyes, the ruff of his neck raised. Merle's mouth went dry when, with a low rumble in his throat, the dog curled its lips back and exposed enormous, yellow fangs. Automatically, she took a step backward, almost falling into the gully she had just crawled out of.

'I see you don't, so you had better get going, lady,' the rancher warned.

'Of . . . of course, I—I'm sorry,' she stammered, her eyes skittering to the man, then riveting back on the dog. Laddie Boy? Killer would have been a better name: she had never seen such a vicious looking animal. Laddie Boy growled a little louder, and Merle quickly side-stepped into the gully, keeping one eye on the dog. With more haste than grace, Merle stumbled her way back to the barbed wire fence, constantly checking over her shoulder to see if the dog was following. On the other side, she broke into a run, not slowing her pace until she reached the safety of the truck.

Once inside the cab of her truck, her heartbeat settled back to normal and her brain started to clear. As it did, a slow burning fury started flowing through her. She slammed her fist against the steering wheel of the truck. 'Damn him!' she swore. Leon! Leon was the one behind this. He was the one who had told the rancher to scare her off the property. And it had worked! There was no way she was going to risk meeting up with Laddie Boy again.

Her temper had cooled only slightly when she went to the truckstop for her meal that evening. She had wasted most of the day tracking down the owner of the hilltop to be certain she at least had his permission to use it as an observation post. Even though he had granted her request, she was still angry. The hill was over a half a mile from the site and was a poor substitute for a closer position. But, given the lie of the land surrounding the well, it was the only option she had.

She was munching on a hamburger, occupying her mind by thinking of all the tortures she would devise for Leon Crane if she ever had him in her power, when the object of her thoughts entered the café. Without hesitation, he strolled over to her table. A smile curved his lips and amusement added a glint to his eyes as he slid into the seat opposite her. Merle had just been imagining that face contorted with pain as she slowly turned the crank on a medieval torture rack, and started to choke on a piece of meat.

Leon quickly shoved a glass of water into her hand, and Merle had to take a large swallow to clear her throat. When she finally gained enough control to look up and glare at him, her face was flushed. 'This table is occupied,' she said coldly.

'Of course it is. We're sitting here,' Leon said pleasantly. He lifted his hand and motioned to the waitress to bring him a cup of coffee.

'I was sitting here first. Would you please leave?' Merle demanded through tight lips.

'No, I feel like having company,' he replied mildly, his attention on the waitress weaving her way through the tables with his coffee. Merle noticed his eyes narrow appreciatively as he scanned the young woman's legs. When the girl reached them, Leon whispered something to her Merle didn't catch. The waitress threw back her head and laughed, winking broadly at him before leaving the table.

Merle's chest was so tight with anger she could hardly breathe. If he was so hard up for company, why didn't he go chat up the waitress and leave her alone? At least the woman would appreciate his presence. She would have loved to make some cutting remark, but her brain was filled with fury. Digging her nails into the palms of her hands, she had to content herself with a vengeful stare.

'Have a bad day, Merle?'

'You know I have,' she choked out.

His eyebrows lifted and his lips pursed in mock sympathy. 'Poor girl. Well, just tell Uncle Leon all about it.'

'Is there any need?' she retorted. 'You know what happened. You're the one responsible. You had that guy with that . . . that *beast* throw me off his property.'

'Beast? Oh,' he laughed, 'you mean Laddie Boy? What's the matter, don't you like animals?'

Merle was absolutely speechless. Her mouth opened and closed convulsively, her head pounded as her blood pressure shot up. If there had been a gun on the table at that moment, she knew she would have used it on him. *Anything* to wipe that look of gloating from his face.

Suddenly she knew if she didn't get away from him she would lose complete control. Knowing Leon, it would only add to his amusement if he managed to goad her into creating a public scene. With jerky movements, she stood up, pushing her chair back. Her temper was held by such a fine thread, it was fortunate that she didn't hear his soft chuckle as she stalked away. She would have completely disgraced herself.

As it was, she almost did, but luckily, regained her

sanity before she did something she would have regretted. Leon's Ferrari was parked directly opposite her Blazer in the truckstop parking lot. For one sweet moment, she considered the pleasure of ramming the sports car with her four-wheel drive. The Blazer was sturdily built and wouldn't sustain much damage, especially compared to what would happen to the Ferrari.

Only when she forced herself to consider the possible consequences of such an action was she able to prevent it. She had underestimated Leon once already, assuming his reasonableness was a sign of weakness. But she didn't think he would remain reasonable if she damaged his precious car. Even though he drove it around on dusty, prairie roads all day, he somehow managed to keep the black paintwork gleaming.

Rage was still churning through her veins when she got back to the motel a few minutes later. It was unfortunate that Greg Larson had chosen this moment to return and was waiting for her when she reached the door to her room.

As Merle recognised him leaning against the door to her room, she saw red. She was almost as angry with *him* as she was with Leon. Since Leon had told her what the geologist had said about her out at the site, she had become conscious of the looks the drillers gave her whenever she went into the truckstop and they were there. So far, none of them had said anything to her, but she expected it was only a matter of time before one of them made a move towards her.

'What are you doing here?' she demanded aggressively when she reached him.

Greg looked slightly taken aback, but answered her. 'I came to see you.'

'And what makes you think I would want to see you?'

'Merle, what's the matter?' he asked bewildered. 'I thought you would be happy to see me. I wouldn't have left at all except Crane fired me and I had to find another job. I came back because . . .' he hesitated, then stumbled on, 'you know I love you.'

'Love me?' Merle scoffed. 'I suppose that's why you spread all those lies about me?'

His face flamed and he lowered his head to stare at his shoe. 'Merle, I know I . . . shouldn't have said all those things, but . . .' He looked up at her, his expression childishly defiant. 'All the guys knew I was dating you. I didn't want them to think that . . . that you . . .'

'So you told them we were having a passionate love affair, is that it?'

'Oh, Merle, when they found out you were a scout, they started saying the only reason we were going together was because you were trying to get information from me. I knew that wasn't true, but . . .' Merle's mouth moved impotently. Was he *that* stupid or did his ego just not allow for rejection? She still hadn't decided which it was, when he continued, '. . . those guys just wouldn't understand. I'm not blaming you for wanting to wait until after we're married, but most people don't these days and——'

'After we're *what*!' Merle interjected, appalled.

'Well, I know we've never actually talked about it, but it is understood.' He stepped over to her and put his hands on her shoulders. Merle stared at him in frozen disbelief as he smiled at her. 'That's why I'm here. I found another job and I came to get you. I've got the licence with me. Tomorrow, we'll drive into Medicine Hat and get married as soon as the courthouse opens.' When he saw her expression, he quickly added, 'You did say once that you didn't like big weddings, so there's no reason to wait.' He started to move his head to kiss her, and she jerked out of his hold.

'Oh, no . . . oh, no,' Merle was shaking her head and raising her hands to ward him off. 'I'm not marrying you. You can forget that idea right now.'

'Merle, I know you're angry with me about those rumours at the site, but try to understand my position. I had to work with those guys, be one of them. They couldn't understand the type of relationship we have . . . that a man and a woman can have more than just sex between them. Be fair, Merle. They would have resented me if they had found out the true depth of our feelings for one another.'

Merle could only stare at him incredulously. He must be mad!

'But you'll see, once we're married it won't seem important anymore,' he continued. Merle backed against the door to her room, her upraised hands preventing him from taking her in his arms. 'My new job, Merle . . . it's an office job, I won't have to leave you to go out in the field . . . they might even be able to find something for you, too. We'll buy a house, you'd like that, wouldn't you? We can be together. We love each other, don't let a little disagreement keep us apart.'

He made a move towards her, and Merle slipped away from him to stand in the centre of the hall. His eyes pleaded with her to understand as he looked at her.

Her previous anger was completely buried under an avalanche of remorse. 'I'm very sorry, Greg, but the only reason I was dating you was because you were the field geologist. The men at the site were right; I was just seeing you in order to get information about the well,' she said, totally unable to meet his eyes. Merle had never felt so despicable in her whole life as she saw the colour slowly drain from Greg's face. But he had to know the truth, half measures wouldn't do. After learning that he had actually gone so far as to buy a marriage licence on the basis of their somewhat shaky friendship, she was certain that he would go right on hoping if she tried to let him down easily.

'But you love me, you must love me,' he insisted, making a movement towards her.

Merle quickly stepped back. 'No, I'm sorry, I don't. I was just using you.'

He stared at her for a long minute, his colour returning in a crimson tide. 'You were using me?' he asked harshly, yet his voice still held a tone that pleaded for denial of the truth.

It was Merle's turn to stare down at her shoe. 'I know it was a rotten thing to do but I didn't realise you were getting in that deep. It's——'

'That deep!' he shouted angrily. 'I lost my job on account of you, you *bitch*! Crane warned me about you, but I was so besotted with you, I didn't want to believe him.' He unleashed a stream of invectives. 'I'm glad I said all those things about you at the site. I'm glad they all think you're a *whore*. I should never have let you get away with holding me off.'

Merle cringed in humiliation. She could hear someone moving down the hall towards them and felt sick inside—all they needed was an audience. She looked up, wondering if there was any way of stemming Greg's angry tirade.

'You're not going to get away with this!' he shouted. His hand shot out and slapped her across the face

Merle staggered back under the force of the blow, tears of pain springing to her eyes. Greg looked murderous as he took a step forward, his arm raised to administer another blow. It was caught just as he was swinging it downward.

'That's enough of that, Larson,' Leon said harshly, pinning Greg's arms behind him. Greg let loose with a string of curses, but Leon held him firmly. 'She isn't worth it, Larson, so calm down. I'm not going to let you beat her up.' Gradually, Greg started to relax, his colour returning to normal. Finally, when he was sure Greg was no longer violent, Leon released him. 'You'd better leave. Go back to Calgary and forget you ever met her. She's not worth going to jail over.'

Greg eyed him condemningly, then turned to glare at Merle. She shrank under his malevolent stare, his face filled with hate. At last, he turned and stalked away. Merle's eyes followed his retreating back as it moved down the hall, guilt gnawing at her gut. She caught her lip between her teeth. It was all her fault, she should never have let him get that involved.

'How's your eye?'

Merle turned to look back at Leon, her hand going to the swelling that was forming at the top of her cheekbone. 'It's okay,' she demurred.

'You're going to have a shiner.'

'I suppose I deserve it.' She glanced down the hall to the door Greg had gone through.

'Probably,' Leon said drily, 'but he shouldn't have done it even so. I don't have much respect for a man who hurts women.' Her eyes flew to his, finding them unreadable. 'You should put some ice on that,' he advised, then turned and walked off, disappearing into a door at the end of the hall near the vending machines.

Over the next week, Merle devoted herself to her job, trying to get that ugly scene with Greg out of her mind. At first it wasn't easy to banish the terrible guilt she felt about the way things had turned out, but as the week wore on, her job and the problems she was encountering drove everything else from her mind. Leon was not just making it difficult to scout the well but nearly impossible. At first, Merle didn't quite realise what was happening. But when four days passed and she noticed she hadn't obtained a depth estimate on the well since her dinner with Leon, she started getting suspicious. She usually managed to count the sections that came out of the hole two or three times during the course of a week. Normally, this was when they were brought out to change the bit, but she hadn't seen the bit being changed since before the breakdown. Nor had they conducted any tests that required bringing up the drill stem.

It was possible that she was just having a bout of bad luck. After all, she didn't spend all her time at the well site. In a normal day, she checked it briefly every three or four hours and if nothing appeared to be happening, she went back to the motel, going for a swim or reading until it was time to check it again. Thus, the drilling pipe could have been brought up several times in the past few days without her seeing it.

But intuition told her it wasn't bad luck. Leon was behind this, and when she overheard a disjointed conversation on the mobile phone referring to 'Wild Rose' she knew he was. *She* was Wild Rose and someone was reporting her movements to the site. Obviously they were waiting until she was safely ensconced at the motel before changing the bit. That Leon knew when she was watching was further confirmed when she saw him throw a mocking salute in her direction one afternoon after she had been lying in position for several hours, fruitlessly waiting for the drill stem to come up.

Merle started spending more time on the hilltop, but it was two days before it looked like her vigilance would pay off. She had just timed the descent of the kelly and jotted it in her notebook, when she trained the spotting scope on the pit of drilling mud that had been pumped from the well. For several minutes she stared at it until she was positive that she was seeing what she thought she was. At last she lowered the scope, convinced that there had been a faint rainbow effect on the surface of the mud.

'Bingo,' Merle whispered to herself. Although it was a rare occurrence, occasionally oil from a bearing layer would enter the mud stream that was pumped from the hole and, thus, created a rainbow effect on the surface of the mud pit. As she considered the implications of this, Merle knew it was essential that she derive some estimate on the hole depth. There was only one thing she could do. She would have to stay here until they brought the pipe out, but at least it should be soon. Once the site geologist noticed the rainbow, he had various test options open to him, most of which required the removal of the drill stem from the hole.

Six hours later, Merle was still on the hilltop, having lowered the scope for the umpteenth time that afternoon. That rainbow was there! Why weren't they doing anything about it? She had watched Leon and the new field geologist go over to examine the pit several times in the last few hours. Though they had picked up some rock samples that had been brought up in the drilling mud, they hadn't ordered any tests in the hole or even stopped the drilling momentarily. Was Leon so determined to stop her from finding out about the well that he was deliberately ignoring this indication of oil? It didn't make any sense. Something fishy was going on. Her lips pressed tightly together and she resolved she wasn't budging until they pulled the stem out.

CHAPTER FIVE

IN the end, she did move. Once. She returned to the Blazer and took out one of the sleeping bags, as well as all the food and drink she could find. A packet of crackers, two candy bars, and a can of warm beer was hardly an adequate supper, but Merle was determined nothing would drive her from the hilltop until she knew what was going on down at the site.

It was one of the longest nights Merle had ever spent. The weather co-operated, but the gentle summer night was marred by the presence of millions of mosquitoes and blackflies and unfortunately, there hadn't been any insect repellant in the Blazer. From the amount of blood the little beasts were extracting from her, Merle judged she would be just about dry by morning. Her legs were covered by the sleeping bag, but her face was exposed, and the thin cotton sleeves covering her arms provided little protection from the insects. Nevertheless, she was determined to maintain her surveillance of the well and refused to give in and snuggle into the folds of the sleeping beg. At least she wasn't in any danger of falling asleep as long as the little perishers kept buzzing around her.

Several hours later the sun came up and the insects departed with the night. Without their intruding presence, Merle found it more and more difficult to stay awake, even though the itch from their bites provided a certain amount of diversion.

It was mid-morning when the drillers finally started pulling the drill stem from the hole. Merle knew her estimate would be nearly useless in judging at what depth the oil had come from given the number of hours that had lapsed since she had first noticed the slick. She was up here now because she wasn't going to give in to Leon Crane.

He came out of the office just after the bit had been changed and the rig workers had started lowering the drill stem back into the hole. Merle had entered the number of sections in her notebook and was preparing to re-roll the sleeping bag when she noticed him. He was carrying a large cardboard box and stopped with it by the big, blue garbage container that serviced the site. He set the box on the ground next to the container and scanned the hilltop, as though searching for her. As if he had willed her to do so, Merle locked her gaze on to him.

Leon stooped down and, opening the box, picked out two metal cans and tossed them into the garbage receptacle. He repeated the action several times and reluctantly Merle raised her binoculars, a cold chill seeping through her. Leon was throwing away empty oil cans.

In a frozen trance, Merle watched him return to the office and emerge with another box, identical to the one he had just emptied. As he threw away the first cans from the box Merle laid the binocular aside. She opened her notebook to the recording she had made of the rate of drop of the kelly just before she had seen the rainbow. It had been slow. She had discounted it, assuming they were faking the drop to confuse her.

Now she knew why they hadn't ordered any tests. For the first time since she was a small child, Merle buried her head in her hands and wept.

The concrete patio that surrounded the pool was

scorching under his bare feet and Leon squinted his eyes against the glare of the midday sun off the water. Thank God the Ferrari had air conditioning. He wouldn't want to have to make the long drive into Calgary this afternoon without it. After his swim, he would have lunch then get started. He had wasted too much time on this project already.

Striding to the edge of the pool, Leon dived cleanly into its sparkling waters. With powerful strokes he swam his laps, making the turns with racing dives.

Hopefully, that little trick with the oil yesterday had convinced Merle Halliday she was wasting her time and he wouldn't have to bother coming back out to the site. Lord, but she was obstinate. He had hoped his little talk about rape, especially after it had been reinforced by that scene with Larson, would have sent her scurrying back to Calgary. Unfortunately, she seemed more afraid of that stupid dog than she did of anything else. At least, Laddie Boy was keeping her on the hilltop and not on their doorstep.

His laps finished, Leon turned on to his back and floated, grinning up at the expanse of blue sky overhead. He had never seen anyone so angry as Merle had been that day in the truckstop after meeting Laddie Boy. It was a wonder she hadn't had a stroke.

That little scene with Greg Larson when she got back to the motel hadn't been very funny though, he thought, his good humour rapidly fading. He had been half-afraid something like that might happen after the way the geologist had so obstinately refused to give her up. He hoped she had enough sense to stay away from the rest of his men. He had only been half-serious when he had given her that little rape speech, but he was beginning to think he might not have been far wrong. Merle was a strange woman. She wasn't that much to look at, but something about her aroused primitive passions. He wasn't a schoolboy when it came to women, but it hadn't been that easy to maintain control that afternoon out on the prairie when she had reponded to him like that. He had been very tempted to roll out one of those sleeping bags—whether that was what she had wanted or not.

He floated to the edge of the pool and flipped over to pull himself out. The chlorinated water ran in rivulets down his chest as he reached for the towelling robe he had dropped by the poolside. As he was rubbing his hair, he glanced around the pool area, his eyes coming to rest on a pair of long, shapely feminine legs stretched out on a lounger opposite him, their owner lying motionless on her stomach. Now what was she doing here? He would have expected her to spend the day in bed, or better yet, to drive back to Calgary and give up the job.

She must have been there all along. She was probably pretending to be asleep so she could ignore him. The thought that she might be trying to avoid him appealed to his sense of humour and he started to grin. He hadn't expected her to be dumb enough to stay out all night watching the well. Once she realised they weren't doing any tests, Leon had expected her to know she had been tricked and give up.

You're a real bastard, Leon, he told himself as he stood up. Shrugging on the robe, he walked around the pool towards the reclining figure. He just couldn't resist the temptation to go over and tease her. She must have felt pretty foolish when she realised what he had done.

His bare feet were soundless on the concrete as he padded over to her. Reaching the lounger where she lay, he stared down at her, letting his eyes roam over

her exquisitely curved female shape. He had always
liked women with good legs, and Merle had a
beautiful pair. The rest of her wasn't bad either, he
thought, his eyes moving over her shapely hips, then
following the narrow curve of her waist.

Leon frowned when he noticed her arms. They were
covered with calamine lotion, the chalky pink failing to
conceal the raised splotches of hundreds of insect
bites. She must have been eaten alive out there last
night. The little fool!

He reached down and removed the wide straw hat
that covered her head. Her face was turned to the side
and was, like her arms, covered in pink calamine.
When she didn't stir, he realised she really was asleep.
He felt a strange little ache in his chest as he studied
her. Her long, dark lashes rested on cheeks distorted
by the bites. Blue shadows ran under eyes that were
faintly red and swollen, one still slightly discoloured
by a fading bruise.

She'd been crying, he thought, mildly shocked. It
had never occurred to him that that might be her
reaction to his little joke. Mad enough to chew nails,
maybe, but tears? That just didn't seem like the Merle
he was coming to know. He felt uncomfortable that
something he had done had reduced her to weeping.
She took her job far too personally, far too seriously.
It was only a game; certainly not worth crying over.

He became aware of the sun beating on his head,
that his hair was already dry from the heat. He should
wake her up, she couldn't sleep out here all day. If she
did, she would have sunburn to contend with in
addition to the bites. He reached down and shook her
gently by the shoulder. 'Merle ... Merle, wake up.
You can't sleep out here.'

Her nose wrinkled faintly, but her lashes never

stirred. The little idiot probably didn't sleep at all last night, he thought, irritated by her stubbornness. A beach robe was lying on the cement next to the lounger and he picked it up, checking the pocket. As he expected, he found her room key and pulled it out. She was dead to the world, so he would have to carry her to her room.

Leon's arms were beginning to ache, his breathing was somewhat laboured, by the time he got her into her room and deposited her on the bed. Merle might have a beautiful shape, but she was no lightweight. He had nearly dropped her while trying to open the door with her key—though he was starting to think that she probably would have slept through even that.

As on that first time he had seen her, her bikini top had been unclasped, so rather than fasten it, he had simply wrapped the robe around her sleeping form to carry her into the building. Now, as she lay reclining on the bed, it fell from her, exposing her firm, rounded breasts. Leon found his eyes drawn to them, the creamy, untanned flesh where the bra top protected them, the dark rose nipples. Desire stirred in his groin. She must have just about driven poor Larson half out of his mind with wanting. No wonder he had wanted to beat her when he found out how little he meant to her.

A flimsy peach nightgown lay on the floor next to the bed, and Leon stooped to pick it up. It seemed a shame to cover her up, but he doubted she would appreciate it if she woke up to find him making love to her. None the less, he couldn't resist tasting the honey of those breasts just once before pulling the nightgown over them and he groaned silently as he felt the nipple harden between his lips. Merle stirred slightly, moaning softly in her sleep, but didn't waken. God, he wanted her, but he forced himself to pull the gown the rest of the way down and tuck her under the covers.

The temptation to join her in the bed was strong, so he made himself look around the room in order to forget it. What a mess! Merle might be a good oil scout, but she wasn't much of a housekeeper. A pile of dirty laundry occupied one corner and every surface was covered with clutter. He knew the motel sent a maid in to the rooms let on a weekly basis twice a week to vacuum and change the bedding and he wondered what the poor woman thought of this.

A stack of books rested on the table by the window and, idly, Leon went over to examine them. *The Prairie Environment, Wild Flowers of Alberta, The World Around You,* smiling to himself, Leon silently read the titles. Opening the flyleaf of the first one, he realised it was a library book, overdue at that. He studied the date stamped on the card. She must have driven into Medicine Hat and picked these up the day after he had questioned her about being a naturalist.

Curious now, he wandered about the room, occasionally picking up an item and examining it. There was a vase of dead flowers on the dresser, half-filled with slimy green water. He wondered if they were the ones she had picked that afternoon he had seen her out on the prairie, his eyes drawn back to the bed.

Realising his thoughts were straying into dangerous territory again, he wandered into the bathroom. Having seen the bedroom, he was not surprised to find cosmetics strewn haphazardly over the vanity, blots of toothpaste splattering the sink. Chuckling softly, he picked up the uncapped tube of toothpaste. If Merle ever got married, the fellow had better be wealthy: he would have to hire plenty of servants to pick up after her.

Putting down the toothpaste, he spotted a bottle of red capsules among the clutter on the vanity. Frowning, he picked it up and read the label: sleeping pills. Automatically, he glanced through the open doorway at the girl on the bed, a cold knot forming in his stomach. She wouldn't have, would she? He knew she was tired after her night on the prairie so it wouldn't be surprising that he had been unable to wake her. Besides, she just wasn't the type. But, she wasn't the type to cry, either, he reminded himself, and she *had* been crying.

He reread the label on the pill vial. The prescription had been for fifty capsules and there were still a large number remaining. He shook the bottle trying to judge how many. He couldn't. He would have to count them, he just couldn't walk out of here without being certain.

Leon cleared away a space on the counter and dumped out the tablets. Carefully, he started counting the little red pills and returning them to the bottle. One, two, three, four . . . Sweat broke out on his brow and he wiped it away impatiently. Forty, forty-one, forty-two, forty-three. He put the last capsule into the vial. Seven missing. He stared at the bottle. She could have taken the seven at any time. Surely, if she had wanted to kill herself she would have taken more? Seven wouldn't be a lethal dose . . . would it?

He looked at the jumble of jars and tubes that littered the vanity. It was possible she had taken the seven by accident. The care and efficiency she devoted to her job obviously didn't extend to the other areas of her life. Merle wasn't very good at taking care of herself and he wouldn't put it past her to accidentally overdose.

Leon had just decided to make another attempt at

trying to wake her, when he spotted something red lying half-hidden by the lid from a jar of face cream. He lifted the lid, frowning at the capsule. Quickly, he began sorting through the bottles and jars lying on the vanity. Within a few minutes, he had discovered three more tablets, one from the floor. That made four out of the seven. Even if she had taken the other three today, he doubted that they would harm her.

He glared at the girl sleeping peacefully on the bed, angry that she had given him such an unnecessary scare. Granted, it was his own fault for jumping to conclusions, but he still wanted to shake her awake and give her a piece of his mind. Instead, he pocketed the vial of sleeping pills. He didn't think she would miss them from amid all the junk and he knew he would feel a lot better if she didn't have them. Not that he thought she would attempt suicide, but he knew he would worry about her accidentally taking too many if he left them.

Quietly, he let himself out of the room and went to prepare for his trip to Calagary. He never did figure out why he stopped at the desk on his way out and arranged for them to have the maid go in to clean Merle Halliday's room every day instead of bi-weekly. He asked them to tell her it was a change in policy and not mention he was having the service charged to Puma Resources. It was a crazy thing to do, especially when he fully expected her to check out and go home as soon as she had rested.

When Merle finally woke, the room was in complete darkness. She felt considerably better after the rest, as she had been exhausted when she had returned to the motel that morning. Too tired to sleep even. Finally, she had taken a sleeping pill and gone for a swim while she waited for it to take effect. Strange, she could remember stretching out on one of the loungers for a few minutes before going back to her room but she couldn't remember leaving the pool area.

She reached over and snapped on the bedside light, propping herself against the headboard. This morning, after finding out what a rotten trick Leon had played on her, she had been half-way resolved to giving up. What information she had managed to gather in the past week was so sketchy as to be nearly useless.

Now that she was rested though, she knew she wasn't going to quit, mainly because she didn't want Leon to know he was getting to her. Also, she was going to control her temper in the future, and not let him goad her as he had been doing.

He couldn't keep up the tactics of this last week indefinitely. He couldn't afford to. In order to make sure she wasn't around when they were changing the bits, he must have being doing it more frequently than necessary so they wouldn't get caught with a worn bit. Drill bits were by no means cheap, so this last week must have cost him.

There were other reasons the drill stem had to come out of the hole, as well. If the bit hits a steeping dipping rock strata the hole will move out of the vertical line. Consequently, 'straighthole' surveys are necessary occasionally to correct deviations. Then, of course, some of the tests required changes in bit or pipe type, so the drill stem had to come up. No, Merle concluded, Leon couldn't continue drilling crooked holes with new bits and not conducting any tests forever.

Though the memory of the 'rainbow defeat' hovered like a black cloud on the edge of her consciousness, Merle attacked her job with renewed vigour over the next couple of weeks. Leon Crane was no longer in evidence, though the field geologist he had hired to replace Greg Larson was staying at the motel. If she had thought she would have had any success she would have tried starting a friendship with him, but concluded it would probably be a waste of time. The new man was a completely different type from Greg and Merle didn't think her feminine wiles would take her very far. He was at least twenty years older than Greg and also wore a wide gold wedding band.

Merle was spending almost all her waking hours on the hilltop now. The one time she noticed her room seemed a little cleaner than usual, she imagined it was because she wasn't spending enough time in it to dirty it up. It was a physically demanding time. The dry heat of the prairie sapped her energy and she continued to lose weight. She suspected her movements were still being monitored, so occasionally she got up before dawn to walk the seven miles to the site so her truck could remain parked at the motel.

Each clue, each little bit of information, was a hard-won victory but slowly she was starting to build a picture of what they were finding underground, and she knew the energy she was expending was worth it. Leon Crane hadn't got the best of her yet.

One day when a shiny-red Blazer drove on to the site, Merle did not connect the truck with Leon at first. But, when it was parked in the shade of the office trailer and he got out, she knew he had changed vehicles. For the first time in three weeks, Merle thought of Leon without feeling a surge of anger. The Leon she had had dinner with the night he had mentioned his interest in her Blazer seemed like a completely different man from the one who had tricked her by dumping oil in the mud pit. Oh, she had glimpsed that mocking humour then, that determination to have his own way, but all his humour hadn't been sarcastic, all his requests domineering. It had been fun to tease him about his accent and he had taken it good-naturedly. Their conversation had been interesting, also. It was surprising how many interests they shared.

For some reason, a lump formed in her throat and she lowered her binoculars and swallowed hard to get rid of it. It would have been nice if they could have just gone on from there; if the well didn't exist.

The midday sun was scorching, burning through the thin cotton of her shirt and plastering it to her back with sweat. There had been thunder showers yesterday and more were forecast for today, but for now, the recent rain had only increased the humidity without the saving grace of providing even one cloud to blot out the fierce rays of the sun. Wiping perspiration from her eyes, Merle picked up the glasses and followed Leon's movements around the site. He walked with long, pantherish strides. First to talk to the rig foreman, then he went over to inspect the 'shaleshaker', the vibrating screening device that separates out the rock samples brought up in the drilling mud. After picking up a few samples, he went to the office, pausing at the door to wave a hand in the direction of the hilltop.

The gesture broke the sentimental spell that had held her while she had watched him, and she gritted her teeth in anger. Someday, someday, she would figure out a way to get even with that man.

Trying to forget the man in the office, Merle rummaged in her knapsack for the tuna sandwich she had got from the truckstop before coming out today. You decided you weren't going to let him get to you, she reminded herself as she picked off the limp lettuce from the warm sandwich. Leon would love nothing better than to goad her into a towering rage, so she just wasn't going to give him the satisfaction. If she had the misfortune of running into him while he was on this visit, she would remain cool and in control.

Leon remained in the office over the next couple of hours and Merle found herself slipping into a doze. She had found an all-night laundromat and had been out until after midnight last night catching up on her laundry. She was glad Leon had fired Greg. She could just imagine him expecting her to wash his clothes, too, she thought, as her eyelids fluttered shut.

When Merle opened her eyes again, great cumulous clouds were building on the horizon and she knew she should start back to the Blazer. Merle had no desire to be caught in a downpour, especially as it would undoubtedly be accompanied by lightning. She wasn't particularly afraid of storms, but only a fool would court disaster. As she was gathering up her belongings, she saw a truck pull up to the entrance of the site. She recognised it immediately as the company truck from a firm that supplied special testing equipment to rigs. Storm or no storm, she would have to stay here now.

Pulling out her spotting scope, Merle watched the truck drive through the gate and park near the rig. The driver got out and was walking towards the office when Leon and the new geologist came out to greet him. She trained the scope on the truck, waiting to see what equipment would be removed from it. The breeze picked up, drying the perspiration on her shirt, as the driver continued his conversation with the other two.

'Come on,' Merle urged them. The storm was

approaching quickly and she wanted to see the truck unloaded before it broke. A fat drop of moisture landed on her back and she saw Leon look up towards the hill. He said something to the driver and then the three people turned away from the truck and went to the office.

Oh, hell!

The first drop was quickly followed by a second, then a third, and then the heavens opened up. Within seconds, Merle was soaked. She had a nylon slicker in her backpack and she pulled it out and draped it over her head. There wasn't much point in putting it on properly as her clothes were already soaked, and at least using it this way provided a sense of shelter. Thunder boomed overhead and she cringed. It would be a miracle if she wasn't struck by lightning but it was probably safer to stay where she was than try to make it back to the truck.

The only advantage of a storm with such violence was that it couldn't last for long. When Merle pulled the slicker off her head twenty minutes later, it had moved on. On the horizon, a perfect rainbow arched against the prairie sky, the bands of colour almost tangible enough to touch. Merle couldn't appreciate its beauty though, reminding her as it did of that earlier defeat on the hill.

Merle shivered slightly, wondering how she could have been so hot only minutes earlier. Though the sun had come out again, a fresh breeze blew across the land, chilling her soaked clothing. There wasn't anything she could do about it now as the door to the office trailer opened and Leon and the others came out to unload the truck.

Fortunately, they unloaded quickly and Merle was soon heading back to her vehicle, the details of the various pieces of equipment she had seen emerge from the truck carefully noted in her journal. Her shirt had dried on her back under the influence of the hot sun, but her jeans were still sodden and uncomfortable, chaffing her inner thighs as she walked. Her nose prickled and she knew she had probably caught a cold as a result of this adventure.

She was about a quarter of a mile from the Blazer when Merle looked up to see Leon striding towards her. Her heart made a quick descent to her toes. It was typical of him to show up just when she was so wet and miserable. Though she was in no mood for his sarcastic taunting of her predicament, she stopped and waited for him to reach her.

'Where have you been?' Leon demanded, coming to a halt in front of her.

For a full minute, Merle stared at him in surprise. Expecting his mockery, his anger caught her completely off guard. Then, she suddenly realised what it was. He knew she had seen the truck. Good Lord, what was he doing now—checking the weather reports before scheduling activities at the site? 'Where do you think?' she taunted.

His eyes swept over her, his lips pulling into a straight line as he noticed her damp jeans. 'You little fool! You're not safe to let out on your own. Didn't you see the storm coming up? What were you trying to do? Get yourself killed?'

'Disappointed I didn't?' she asked sweetly.

At the furious light that flamed in his eyes, Merle shrank away from him. 'No job is worth risking your life for! Why didn't you move when you saw the storm coming?'

'You'd have liked that, wouldn't you? Then I wouldn't know what was in that truck, but now I do.'

She resisted the childish urge to stick her tongue out at him.

He said something unprintable, then gritted his teeth. 'I don't care about the stupid truck. These prairie storms can be dangerous if you're caught out in the open. You could have been struck by lightning, you . . .' he stopped in exasperation. His hands went to her upper arms and suddenly he pulled her to him, holding her tightly against his chest. 'You have no idea what you put me through these last few minutes. I knew you were up there and there wasn't a damn thing I could do about it.'

'You . . . you were worried about me?' Merle asked him in astonishment.

He eased her away from him slightly, though he didn't release her. Looking down into her face he said, 'Of course I was worried about you. You have to be the biggest idiot I have ever known.' The insult was spoken in the tone of an endearment. He lowered his head, his lips seeking hers. The tenderness of his touch, the gentle movement of his mouth over hers evoked an instant response within her. Her arms slid up his shoulders to wrap around his neck, her fingers tangling in the hair at his nape. She eased herself closer to him, slowly merging her form with his until the space between them disappeared.

His hands moved down her spine, slowly, caressingly, then stopped when they reached her waist. He lifted his head and stared down at her. 'You're wet,' he said flatly. 'I ought to beat you for being so reckless.' He dropped a quick kiss on her parted lips, then, 'Come on, I'll drive you back to the motel. You can give me the keys to the Blazer and I'll have someone bring it in later.' He released her and stooped to pick up the knapsack from where she had dropped it, frowning as he hefted it to his shoulder. 'It's no wonder you've got so skinny if you lug this around with you all the time,' he said disgustedly, his eyes on her loose-fitting jeans.

'Well, thanks a lot,' she snapped. When he was kissing her, she had forgotten how angry she was with him, but she was remembering now. Who did he think he was, anyway? He had played a rotten trick on her and now he expected her to just fall in his arms. Well, he could think again, she thought, abandoning her resolution to keep her temper around him. 'I can find my own way back to the motel, thank you. I'm not going to listen to your sarcastic comments all the way home.' She snatched the knapsack away from him and turned in the direction of her truck.

'For Pete's sake, Merle, stop being so childish.' He caught up with her and grabbed her wrist to keep her from walking on. 'I was just commenting on the fact that I had noticed you have lost a lot of weight over the summer. I was expressing concern.'

'I think you know where you can put your concern,' Merle snapped, pulling her arm free. 'I don't need your kisses, or your concern . . . or *you*!'

His face was pale under his tan, but his eyes were chips of emerald as he looked down at her. A hard knot of pain blocked her throat and her eyes filled with tears. Jerking away from him, she stalked over to her truck. She was never going to let him know he could make her cry.

The chips had been stale, tasting more of rancid oil and salt than potato, none the less she had eaten them. Now, Merle crumpled the empty bag and hurled it across the room in the direction of the wastepaper basket. The missile ricocheted off the dresser and

landed on the floor next to a candy bar wrapper and
several discarded tissues. After draining the last of the
warm, flat Coke from the can, she sent it on a route
similar to that of the potato chip bag, only this time
her aim was better and the can landed in the waste
container with a loud clatter.

She stretched slightly, then settled back against the
pillows propped against the headboard of the bed,
trying to concentrate on the television. The coyote was
assembling an elaborate catapult and since she knew
he still wouldn't catch the roadrunner, the cartoon
didn't succeed in distracting her from the protests of
her stomach.

Finally giving up, Merle got out of bed and
switched the set off just as the coyote was hurtling
towards a bluff. She supposed she couldn't be that ill
if she were hungry, but the thought didn't give her
much comfort. In the past two days, she had only left
her room to visit the vending machines located at the
end of the hallway. Junk food and soda weren't exactly
the recommended diet for a cold sufferer but she had
felt too ill to dress and drive over to the truckstop for a
meal.

In the bathroom, Merle stared in the mirror over
the sink, making a face as she inspected her image.
Her complexion was colourless, and even her eyes
looked faded. Her nose was pink and sore from
constant blowing. She thought you were supposed to
look ethereal and fragile when you were ill: she just
looked sick.

For a few seconds longer, Merle studied her
reflection critically. At least she hadn't started to come
out in spots from all the garbage she had been eating
the last couple of days, but it was time she forced
herself to go out and have a decent meal. Maybe if she

showered and dressed, she would feel better. She really couldn't afford to lie around the motel unit feeling sorry for herself. Work at the well would be going on whether she was there to witness it or not and she would have to go out for a look tomorrow, cold or no cold.

Actually, she did feel better once she had bathed and dressed. As she wasn't going out to the site, she could afford to don something feminine, so she chose to wear the second dress in her wardrobe, a pale blue sleeveless sundress. It had a low neckline and full skirt, and with the application of a light coating of make-up she decided she looked almost human again. Perhaps she would even feel it once she had a hot meal inside her.

CHAPTER SIX

THE café was crowded when she arrived, but there was an empty booth near the entrance and Merle slid into it. She had eaten here so frequently in the past few weeks she didn't bother consulting the menu before giving her order to the waitress. She asked for the house speciality of home-made beef vegetable soup, deciding she would order a sandwich later if she still felt hungry after the soup.

As she waited for the girl to return with her soup and the coffee she had ordered, Merle wondered if it hadn't been a mistake to come out. She had felt well enough when she had left the motel, but now . . .

Leaning her head back against the seat, she closed her eyes. The air conditioning in the café raised goose bumps along her arms and she clamped her teeth together to stop them from chattering. If she had had the energy, she would have left, as the thought of food was no longer appealing. Now she was here though, she supposed she should force herself to eat something.

She sensed someone come to stand by her table, and Merle opened her eyes expecting to see the waitress bringing her order. Instead, Leon was towering over her, a frown puckering his forehead. 'Are you all right, Merle?'

For several seconds she just stared at him in mute surprise. She had been hoping to avoid him. Although, she admitted, he had been genuinely concerned about her having been caught in the storm, she didn't think that would stop him from taunting her about having caught a cold as a result. Irrationally though, she felt a quiver of pleasure that he had stopped to talk to her, and she couldn't suppress the smile that hovered on her lips as he slid into the seat opposite her.

'You don't look very well. Are you ill?' Leon asked, when Merle remained silent.

'Not really, I just have a cold.' As though to emphasise her point, she made a hasty grab for a tissue, barely managing to cover her mouth before a sneeze ripped through her sinuses.

'Bless you.' He was studying her face and Merle felt heat creep into her pale cheeks. She knew only too well that she looked as bad as she felt. Despite her efforts to improve her appearance before coming out, nothing could disguise the rawness around her nose or the lacklustre expression in her eyes.

Her own unhealthy condition was a glaring contrast to his obvious fitness. He was dressed in work clothes, but even the drab olive green didn't detract from the healthy glow of his bronzed skin. The shirt was opened at the neck and, as her eyes rested on the triangle of chest left exposed, she found herself mentally removing the garment. With uncanny clarity, she could picture him as she had seen him at the pool, the firmly muscled torso, the mat of hair that ended in a vee just above his navel.

Aware that the sudden weakness that overcame her had absolutely nothing to do with her cold, Merle quickly looked back at his face. As she met his eyes, she knew he was aware of what she had been thinking. Irritated, Merle reverted to the topic of her cold, snapping waspishly, 'Well, aren't you going to say you told me so?'

Leon grinned. He even has healthy *teeth*, Merle thought petulantly. 'I don't have to, you just said it for me.'

The waitress arrived then, greeting Leon with hearty familiarity. Leon responded in kind, saying, 'Hi, Sally. You're looking especially pretty today.' He slid Merle a look that made her want to hit him, then turned his attention back to the waitress. 'I'll just have coffee.'

'Sure thing, honey.' The woman scurried away to fill the order. Merle looked at Leon, her expression annoyed. She had been eating here regularly for over a month, yet each time she came in the waitress treated her as though she were a total stranger. At first, she had thought it was because of her sex, but after a time she had noticed that Sally treated most of her customers, male or female, with the same impersonal, slightly surly, disdain she did Merle. Merle had concluded that that was just the waitress's personality.

'Honey' has certainly managed to thaw her, thought Merle, her irritation escalating when Sally returned with his coffee only moments later and neglected to bring Merle's own order for coffee and soup. When Merle called her attention to the oversight, she had the distinct impression the girl had forgotten Merle was even sitting there and further more, was annoyed that she had pointed out her lapse in front of Leon.

Finally the girl brought her order and Merle stared down at the bowl of steaming soup, wondering why she had ever wanted it in the first place. She knew her cold wasn't solely responsible for her lack of appetite. The way the waitress had fawned over Leon brought into startling clarity the effect he had on women, herself included. He drew them like flowers drew bees. And even if she wasn't scouting his well, with the number of bees he no doubt had buzzing around him, a common drone like herself didn't have much of a chance. Not that she wanted one, of course, she was forced to remind herself.

'Is there something wrong with the soup?' Leon interrupted her thoughts.

Merle looked up at him, shaking her head. 'No, I guess I'm not as hungry as I thought I was.' She pushed the bowl away.

Leon reached across the table and moved it back in front of her. 'Please, Merle,' he coaxed and Merle felt her breath catch at the tender expression in his eyes, 'your cold will hang on that much longer if you don't eat properly.'

Merle looked down at the soup, wondering what he would say if he knew she had been existing on potato chips and candy bars for the past two days. 'Merle,' his voice took on a sterner note, 'it will be cold if you don't stop procrastinating. Now, eat.'

'I don't see why you should care whether I eat or not,' Merle sulked.

'Of course I care,' Leon assured her, pushing a spoon in her hand. 'Spudding that well isn't nearly as much fun when I know you're not up on your hill watching me.'

'It's all a big game to you, isn't it?' Merle grumbled, but nevertheless took the spoon and dipped it into the bowl. Why was she was letting him order her around like this? She still didn't want the soup. The cold had robbed her of her sense of taste and it could have been made from dishwater for all she knew. After a few spoonfuls, she looked up at Leon wondering if she had eaten enough to satisfy him. His frown told her she hadn't, so with a surprising lack of defiance, she returned her attention to the bowl, not looking up again until it was empty.

'That wasn't so bad, now was it?' he asked as she pushed the empty bowl aside. 'You feel better now, don't you?'

'You sound just like my mother. She used to like to pretend she was Florence Nightingale, too,' Merle said sourly, though she admitted to herself that she did feel better now that she had something in her stomach.

'And you didn't like it?'

She shrugged slightly. 'You'd have to know my mother to understand.' When he just looked at her questioningly, she found herself saying, 'Whenever I was sick as a kid, she fussed all over me, but as soon as I got better, she forgot all about me. My mother is very inconsistent. She's always either trying to run my life, or she forgets she even has a daughter. I used to think if I did things the way she wanted me to, we would get along better. It didn't make any difference, though, so finally I decided to just go my own way.'

'And your way wouldn't happen to be just the opposite to the way she wants, would it?' Leon asked, probing.

'Oh, don't misunderstand,' Merle retracted hastily. How had she let her tongue run away with her like that? 'I'll admit, she's not happy about my career. She thinks I should settle down, but I'm an oil scout because that's what I like doing. It has nothing to do with her. Besides, my childhood wasn't that bad. Mom did the best she could. She had a lot of her own problems to contend with and they sometimes made it hard for her to help me with mine. That's all.' How did they get on to this topic? She never talked to anyone about her mother.

'What do you mean she had her own problems?'

'Oh.' Merle looked away from him. It would be nice if the ceiling would fall in or something so they could change the subject. 'She got married a lot. It didn't usually work out too well, so she was always trying to salvage the situation.'

She was starting to feel extremely embarrassed. Leon could see too easily beneath the words to the emotions they sheltered. She liked to keep her friendships on surface levels—and Leon wasn't even a friend. Or was he? Maybe in some weird way he was. This whole situation was so damn confusing! Suddenly, Merle gathered up her bag, trying to catch Sally's eyes so she could get the bill. 'I think I'll go back to the motel now. I'm kind of tired.'

'Shouldn't you have a bit more to eat first? A bowl of soup is not much of a meal.'

'No, I'm full, honestly.' If he thought she was going to stick around and tell him the story of her life, he was crazy.

He looked doubtfully from her to the empty bowl. 'I know you're probably not feeling that great, but you should be able to manage more than that. Why don't you have a sandwich if you don't want more soup?'

'No! I don't want anything more.' Her tone was sharp and she saw his eyebrows lift as the temperature in his green eyes dropped. Her former irritation had returned full force, though it was more with herself than him.

'If that's all you're having for tea——'

'Look, Leon, I'm an adult, now. I don't need a *nanny*,' Merle said nastily, stressing the British term.

'Don't you?' he asked, his own anger rising to meet hers. 'You obviously can't look after yourself. If you could, you wouldn't have caught that cold in the first place. The only thing that surprises me is that you aren't out there watching that bloody site right now. What happened? Couldn't you drag a hospital bed up the hill?'

'Oh, you'd love it if I forgot all about the well, wouldn't you? Well, don't hold your breath because I'm not going to.' Merle stood up abruptly and peered down at him. 'And now that you mention it, I think I *will* go out and have a look tonight.' With that parting shot, she stalked over to the cash register to pay her bill.

Leon came up behind her as she was waiting for the cashier and reaching past her, tossed a handful of coins on the counter to cover the cost of his coffee. Then, without even looking in her direction, he walked out of the truckstop. Finally, the cashier returned to the cash register. Merle still didn't have her bill, but eventually it was tracked down and she was able to pay for her meal and leave.

During the few minutes delay in her departure, her temper abated and she knew she couldn't possibly carry out her intention to go out to the site. Even if she were dressed for it, she was in no condition to go scrambling around the prairie in the middle of the night. Just coming out for a meal had depleted her small store of energy. No, the site would just have to wait until tomorrow.

Having reached this sensible conclusion, she immediately abandoned it when she saw Leon's Blazer stopped directly behind hers, trapping it in its parking spot. Merle froze in her tracks. So, he thought he could *force* her to stay away from the well site, did he? She wondered how he was going to like having the side of his new Blazer bashed in.

Leaving his truck running, Leon got out and stalked over to her. Wordlessly, he took her by the arm and started pulling her towards his vehicle.

Trying to jerk free, Merle cried, 'What do you think you're doing?'

'I'm taking you back to the motel,' he said firmly. Stopping abruptly, he turned her to face him, his jaw tight with determination. 'I'm tired of playing games with you. The only reason you want to go out to the site tonight is to spite me. Well, I'm not going to let you, so you can stop arguing about it. Behave yourself, and I *might* let you go out tomorrow—provided, of course, that your cold is better.'

Merle's mouth dropped open, momentarily too astonished by the arrogance of his demand to even feel outraged. He took her bag from her and fumbled inside it, then pulled out her truck keys. 'I'll be keeping these until you're well enough to go back to work,' he explained, slipping them into his pocket and starting to propel her towards his truck.

Merle tried to twist away from him, but his hold had her firmly in hand. Finally, she kicked out, catching his shin with her foot.

'You little brat,' Leon snarled, wincing with pain. In one motion, he swung her up into his arms and started to carry her to his Blazer.

'You won't get away with this,' Merle threatened, struggling in his arms and beating his chest with her fists. 'You can't kidnap me!' She threw her head back and started to scream, 'Ra . . .'

His mouth on hers choked off the word. Merle rolled her head from side to side to escape the brutal pressure of his lips on her. He was still carrying her towards the truck, and she tried unsuccessfully to capture his lip with her teeth. He lowered her to the ground, one arm holding her firmly against the length of him, his other hand going to the nape of her neck to hold her head still.

Although his mouth was still firmly on hers, his kiss was no longer punishing and Merle's resistance started to fade. The hard muscles of his chest crushed against her breasts, his thighs pressed against hers. Her hands, which had been clenched into fists, uncurled as she rested them against his shoulders.

Slowly, his hands began to explore her back, moving down her spine to mould her hips closer to his. Gently parting her lips with his tongue, he explored the inner softness of her mouth. Merle moaned softly, arching against him. Wave after wave of warm desire was washing over her, awakening urgent hunger. Her pulse was thundering in her ears as he moved one hand to her breast, gently stroking it through the cotton material of her dress.

He lifted his mouth from hers, and sprinkled light kisses over her face, before easing her away from him. An amused smile curved his lips as he noticed the languid expression in her eyes, the tinge of colour in her cheeks. 'You were saying something about rape?' he teased.

Before Merle could react to his taunt, Leon had bundled her into the Blazer and was putting it into motion. For a moment, Merle fumed in silence but his kiss had crippled her anger and she couldn't restore it to its former intensity. Finally, more in an effort to save face than from emotion, she said shrewishly, 'I hope you get my cold now.'

Leon looked over to her, laughter in his eyes. 'After that kiss, it would be a small price to pay.'

Merle slumped back in her seat and stared out the side window, a smile suddenly twisting her lips. *Just let him think he had won this round.* Of course, she would have to walk back to the truckstop to pick up her Blazer, but it would be worth it just to score off him. He thought he had her because he had taken her keys, but he didn't realise she had a spare set in her room. And even if she couldn't find them, she could still hot wire the Blazer. At one time, she had dated a young man of dubious morals who had taught her how it was done. He had even shown her how to pick the door lock, a handy skill if one happened to lock one's keys inside. Whatever happened to Earl? Prison, probably.

The truckstop was only about two miles from the motel, so within a few minutes Leon had parked and was escorting her to her room. Merle had expected him to leave her then, but he followed her inside despite the lack of an invitation.

'What now, Leon?' Merle asked in a resigned tone, turning to face him. 'You've had your way. You've brought me home, so why can't you just leave me alone?' It would take some time to figure out where she had put the keys and she wanted him out of here so she could start looking for them.

'I will as soon as I've picked up the spare keys.'

Leon's eyes flicked around the room. Even now that she had a daily maid, it wasn't much neater than it had been the first time he had seen it.

'The spare keys?' Merle asked innocently, her spirits plunging. She hoped she could remember everything Earl had taught her.

'That's right.' He grinned at her, then walked unhesitatingly to the dresser and, lifting aside a magazine, picked up the extra set of keys to her vehicle. As he slipped them into his pocket, he turned around to look at her.

Merle's eyes were wide, her lips parted in astonishment. 'How did you do that?' It would have taken her *hours* to find the keys.

'X-ray vision,' Leon explained, drily. A half-believing look flickered across Merle's face so he continued, his expression dead-pan, 'You've discovered my secret, Merle. You see, I am not the mild-mannered oil executive, Leon Crane. In reality, I was born in a galaxy far from earth. I was sent here as a small baby when my own planet was destroyed.'

'I should have known,' Merle admitted, injecting a note of awe into her voice. 'I saw your movie three times.'

'Really? You've seen *Superman* three times?' He came over to her, looping his arms casually around her waist.

'*Superman*?' she asked, her forehead pleating in a frown. 'I was talking about *E.T.*' She tilted her head back to look up at him, barely managing to keep her smile from breaking free.

'Ouch!' Leon winced, laughing, and Merle joined in. 'I walked right into that one, didn't I?' He grinned down at her, then kissed her lightly on the forehead. 'You feel warm. I'd better let you get to bed. I don't suppose you'd invite me to come with you?' he asked, hopefully.

For a long moment, Merle just stared at him. She was tempted, very tempted to say yes. He was so attractive to her, both physically and mentally. Despite the fact that he could make her angrier than any man she had ever known, she knew instinctively that he would take her higher than anyone else ever could. If only they could have met at another time and in another place.

Finally, she shook her head and answered, 'I don't suppose I would.' Her hands were resting on his chest as he held her in the light embrace. She could feel the steady throb of his heart under her palms, the rise and fall of his chest as he breathed. That kiss in the truckstop parking lot was still fresh in her mind and her pulse was hammering. It wouldn't take much pressure from him to make her change her mind, so she slipped out of his hold before temptation overruled good sense. With a few feet between them, Merle found it easier to stand by her decision, though she couldn't help missing the warmth of his arms around her.

Merle looked over to him. She suspected he was well aware of what she was thinking. He gave her one of those mocking looks she was all too familiar with, then bid her good night. As the door clicked shut behind him, Merle sighed, not sure whether it was with relief or regret.

She didn't understand herself anymore. Her desire to defy Leon by going out to the well tonight had been lost somewhere in that light-hearted exchange. She had to admit that her will to defy him on *anything* was becoming seriously impaired. It was rather frightening to think she might actually like his taking charge of her. With another sigh, Merle went to prepare for bed. It wasn't until she was hovering in the edge of sleep several minutes later that she recalled he never did tell her how he knew where her spare keys were.

She awoke after only a few hours' sleep, the rumblings from her stomach deafening in the silent room. Her cold felt much better, but she wished she had had more for supper. If only they hadn't got into that stupid discussion about her mother, she might have stayed and had a sandwich as Leon had wanted her to. But, she really couldn't have Leon as a confidant. She had managed to reach the age of twenty-five without one, and to cast the man she was working against into that role was utterly ridiculous.

Merle switched on the light and rummaged through the litter on her bedside table, checking the discarded potato chip bags for crumbs. Finally, she admitted she would have to go down to the vending machines if she wanted something to eat.

She got out of bed and slipped a robe on over her nightdress. It was one o'clock in the morning and unlikely that anyone would be moving about the hall. Even if they were, the dressing-gown was hardly revealing. The quilted, rust-coloured satin reached her ankles, the high neckline, her throat. Only the rope belt knotted at her waist gave any hint to the shape concealed beneath the folds of the robe.

Taking a pocketful of change with her, Merle let herself out of her room, her slippered feet carrying her soundlessly down the hall to the machines. She dropped the correct number of coins into the candy machine and pulled the knob beneath a chocolate bar. While she was here, she decided she might as well get some soda, and pushed the button for an orange drink after depositing the required coins. The clatter of the can as it came down the chute was thunderous in the silent hallway and Merle flinched.

She retrieved the soda and was turning to go back to her room when she heard a nearby door open. 'Hungry, Merle?' Leon asked, lounging negligently against the doorjamb. He was wearing a navy blue, knee-length velour robe tied at the waist. As Merle's eyes moved over his bare legs beneath the robe, to the expanse of chest revealed by the parted neckline, her heart skipped a beat. The robe was *all* he was wearing, unless you counted the taunting smile that played about his mouth.

'I just thought I'd have a midnight snack,' Merle admitted breathlessly. She couldn't seem to look away from that bared chest. It was deeply tanned, the bonzed flesh sprinkled with curling black hairs. Firm muscles rippled beneath satin skin as Leon straightened and walked over to her.

'Come on. I'll fix you something to eat.' He slipped his arm around her shoulders, taking the candy bar and soda from her. 'From the looks of your room earlier, I'd say you've already had enough junk food for one day. Come into my room and I'll do you some eggs.'

As Merle scooped the last bite of the fluffy, golden omelette Leon had made for her on to her fork, she felt a twinge of envy. The kitchen units at the motel were very comfortable and she wished she had thought to ask for one when she had checked in. There was a long bank of cupboards, providing both work and storage space, a compact fridge, and an electric stove. In addition to a small dining table, the room contained a convertible sofa and an easy chair arranged around the television in one corner to form a cosy sitting area. The bedroom was a separate room with a private bath adjoining it.

Not that she would have been able to keep the unit as clean and neat as Leon did. Her eyes strayed to the gleaming kitchen counters. If she had cooked the meal, she knew they would have been littered with crumbs and egg shells and dirty pans. Leon somehow managed to clean up as he went along and she wished she could be as meticulous.

Merle pushed away her empty plate, smiling across the table at her host. 'Thank you. It was very good.' Though he hadn't eaten, Leon had joined her with a cup of coffee while she ate her meal.

'I told you once I couldn't resist helping a lady in distress,' he dismissed her gratitude, returning her smile without a trace of mockery. She had been expecting him to give her a hard time about being hungry after her refusal to eat at the truckstop earlier, but other than that initial taunt, he hadn't teased her. Now, Leon stood, picking up the dirty dish. 'Why don't you take your coffee over to the couch and I'll take care of this?'

She supposed she should offer to help clean up, but now that she was no longer hungry she felt delightfully drowsy, so she merely followed his suggestion. Setting her cup on the side table, Merle curled up on the sofa to wait for Leon to join her, tucking her legs beneath her.

Although it only took him a couple of minutes to wash the dish and finish tidying the kitchen area, Merle was sound asleep when he went over to the couch. He should have sent her back to her room when she had finished eating and not given into the desire to have her company just a little longer. As he stared down at her, her face slightly pale under its tan, he asked himself again what he saw in her. Not that she was homely, but he certainly knew more beautiful women. Ones with better shapes, too, he admitted, thinking how her curves had suffered with her recent weight loss.

He was asking for trouble by continuing to see her. Apart from anything else, she could create a lot of problems for him on this well. Had already done so, for that matter. But, he sighed, she looked like such a little kid when she slept. And he knew she couldn't take care of herself nearly as well as she thought she could.

Leon reached down and lifted her into his arms, surprised that despite her slenderness she was still quite heavy. She didn't stir and he wondered how anyone could sleep as soundly as Merle did. As he started to carry her from the unit, he thought of the long haul to her room. On impulse, he changed direction and took her to his bedroom.

Merle opened her eyes and stared into smiling green ones. She quickly shut her eyes again, wondering if it was her cold that was causing her to have such a crazy dream. Her eyes flew open again when a movement beside her, followed by the pressure of a very real hand coming to rest on her stomach, told her she wasn't dreaming.

'Good morning,' Leon said pleasantly, as though they had been waking up in the same bed all their lives. 'How does your cold feel this morning?' The hand on her stomach slid upward, over her breast, along her throat, to her forehead. 'Mmm. You don't seem to have a temperature anymore. You must be getting better.'

The hand took the return journey to her midriff, every bit as intimately as it had the first time, while Leon lowered his head to gently nuzzle the bare skin of her throat. Frantically, Merle flipped through her memories of last night, but still couldn't remember getting into bed with Leon. Granted, she had *thought* about it, but thought wasn't deed. 'Leon, why are you in my bed?' she finally asked.

As she asked the question, she realised she was curious rather than angry—and she wasn't angry because she was exactly where she wanted to be. Her grey eyes widened as she watched him lower his head towards hers. Oh, you fool, she chided herself. You should have stayed away from him. You shouldn't have let yourself fall for him because you are going to have a hell of a time stopping this from going any further.

His lips moved along her jaw line, leaving a trail of

light kisses until he was near her ear. 'I'm not,' he whispered, answering her question. 'You're in my bed.' He caught her earlobe between his teeth, gently pulling on it. Merle felt the hand tug her nightgown upwards and slip beneath it. It moved in a slow caress over the bare skin of her belly until it reached her breast. Cupping it gently, Leon kneaded the rounded orb at the same time as his tongue explored the shell of her ear.

Merle twisted her head away, trying to hang on to her sanity. They really shouldn't be doing this! You just didn't do things this way. Making love was supposed to be a rational decision, something you considered, discussed, prepared for, then you decided to move the relationship on to that plane. You just didn't wake up one morning in bed together. It was crazy, it was totally irrational. 'Leon, stop that!' she demanded in an agonised whisper.

He lifted himself on to one elbow and grinned down at her. His hand didn't leave her breast but continued the tender caress, his thumb teasing the nipple. 'I thought you were enjoying it.' He shifted slightly so that his body was pressed against her side. She could feel his arousal, feel that he was naked beneath the covers.

'Leon, please, we can't do this.'

'Why?' He pressed his mouth against the pulse beating rapidly in her throat.

'Because ...' It was hard to think of a reason when heat was coursing through every vein, bringing her senses to life. 'Because we can't. We haven't even talked about it. Anyway, we're ...' The hand was moving again, slowly circling downward. 'We're enemies, Leon. We can't make love.'

'I don't think of you as my enemy.' His breath

fanned her throat as his mouth moved along the curve of her neck. 'Besides, isn't there something in the Bible about loving your enemies?' he asked softly, his lips brushing hers. 'If there isn't, there should be.'

His lips moved sensuously over hers, parting her own with gentle intent. He ran his tongue lightly across the ivory of her teeth as his fingers found their goal. Merle arched her back, the intimacy of his caress destroying the last of her fragile defences. Desire was an aching hunger in the core of her being, a primitive need that could not be denied or ignored.

Merle turned towards him and linked her arms around his neck as she met the demand of his kiss with demands of her own. He groaned softly as the hard nipples of her breasts pressed against his chest, her body becoming fluid as she yielded against him.

Lifting his head a fraction, his lips left her. He felt the tremor that raced along the surface of her skin and whispered, 'My love, let me get rid of this.' Kneeling beside her, he placed his hands at the vee of her nightgown and pulled sharply.

The lace parted easily, but when the tear reached the seam that ran beneath her breasts, it stopped abruptly. Leon looked down at the obstreperous material, his brow meeting in a puzzled frown. As Merle watched the changing expressions flicker across his face, she started to giggle. He threw her a hard look which only served to increase her amusement, sending her into gales of laughter.

'You're a cruel woman, Merle,' Leon scolded her, his expression hurt.

'If you could have seen your face,' Merle choked trying to swallow her laughter.

Leon lay back down beside her and stared at the ceiling. Merle turned her head to look at him, her eyes still dancing with amusement. Her hand reached out to trace his profile, but he didn't turn to her. 'I'm sorry I laughed—but, you're always laughing at me,' she reminded him.

'A man doesn't like being laughed at when he's making love,' he said in a petulant tone.

Merle rolled over and cradled her head against his chest. Had she really hurt his feelings by laughing like that? Leon, of all people, should have seen the humour in the situation. That was one of the things she liked about him. Oh, it was maddening when he laughed at her, but he was usually able to laugh at himself as well. She tugged on her lower lip with her teeth. Of course, men were strange when it came to sex. They had such fragile egos, maybe she really had hurt his feelings.

'I'm sorry, Leon,' she murmured against his chest. Her fingers twined in the dark hair that covered it, stroking the smooth skin underneath. Shockingly, she felt near to tears. So many times she had wanted to hurt him, to shatter his confidence the way he did hers. She couldn't bear having finally done so in this way.

'Well, I might, just might, forgive you, if you'll promise never to wear that damn thing in my bed again,' he said sternly. Rolling over swiftly, he dragged the offending garment off her and threw it to the floor.

When he had turned back to her, Merle stared into his face. Oh, she knew that look! He hadn't been hurt at all, he had just been teasing her. 'You rat!'

She raised her fist to push him away and he snatched her wrist, raising her arm over her head. His mouth sought hers and he whispered huskily against her parted lips, 'Come, dear enemy, let's make love,' before his mouth came down on hers in drugging possession. The rough hair of his chest brushed against the softness of her breasts, igniting primal fires that scorched between them. His lips moved from hers to journey in hungry exploration of the secrets of her body, savouring the taste of her, feeding the flames of passion.

'Please, now,' she pleaded, feeling that she was slowly being driven mad by the urgency of her desire. In wanton demand, she guided him over her, her nails clawing his back as she writhed beneath him. In an explosion of sensation that tore a cry from the very depths of her soul, he claimed her.

CHAPTER SEVEN

MERLE hummed softly to herself as she lifted the slices of bacon from the pan. Leon was in the bedroom dressing and she had offered to make their breakfast. Cooking wasn't a task she normally enjoyed, but she was deriving a great deal of pleasure from preparing this meal.

Awkwardly, she poured out the excess grease from the skillet, then took four eggs from the carton on the counter and broke them into the pan. Next, she loaded the toaster and found two plates in the cupboard. She took the fresh tomato she had found in the refrigerator and cut and arranged the slices on the plates with the bacon.

The counter was littered with egg shells and splatters of grease. Half the contents of the fridge were strewn over its surface. Merle frowned slightly when she saw the mess she had created, wishing she could learn to be as neat as Leon. It would probably take her longer to clean up than it would for them to eat.

Leon came out of the bedroom as she was sliding a spatula under one of the eggs to flip it over and she looked over her shoulder to smile at him. He was dressed in a dark blue business suit and carrying a briefcase. Merle glanced down at the satin robe she was wearing. It was just like in the movies, she thought, with the wife fixing her husband's breakfast before he goes to work. The idea didn't repel her as it once might have. All I need is some rollers in my hair.

She returned her attention to the pan and saw she

had broken the yolk on the egg she had been turning. 'Darn,' she muttered as she attempted to turn another egg, and broke the yolk again. If this were a movie, they would have to do a re-take on the eggs. Someday, she promised herself, she would learn how to cook. She couldn't even fry eggs properly.

Black smoke started to rise from the toaster while she was still occupied with the eggs and Leon hurried over. He removed the toast, and taking it to the sink, started scraping off the black with a dinner knife.

'I'm sorry, Leon. I guess I'm not much of a cook,' Merle apologised softly as she scooped the eggs out on to the plates. The breakfast was ruined, the kitchen wrecked, all because she was hopelessly undomesticated.

He glanced over at her, and seeing her expression, abandoned the toast and went to her. Taking her in his arms, he gathered her to his chest. 'Now don't go weepy on me, Merle,' he chastened her.

'Don't be ridiculous, Leon. I'm not one of those silly women who cry over things,' Merle denied, though she kept her head buried in his chest.

He tilted her face up to his, noting the soft mist in her grey eyes. Poor, silly Merle, he thought, dropping his head to plant a hard kiss on her mouth. Her lips clung to his and she pressed closer to him. Leon laughed softly, hugging her tightly before putting her from him. 'When you can kiss like that, Merle, you don't need to worry about what kind of cook you are,' he assured her, enjoying the surge of colour that raced up her cheeks as she realised he knew she had been close to tears.

A few minutes later, they were seated at the table eating their breakfast. The toast tasted scorched and the coffee was a little too strong, but the eggs were delicious, even if they didn't look it. Though they ate in silence, their eyes met frequently in intimate communication. At each glance from Leon, Merle felt a little surge of warmth, a percolating happiness that seeped through her veins.

'Merle,' Leon said, pushing away his empty plate and pouring them more coffee, 'I have to be in Calgary this afternoon. I've got a meeting. Come with me.'

'To Calgary?'

'Yes. I don't want to be away from you.' He reached over and twined his fingers with hers. 'Please come, Merle. We'll have a beautiful time. The Stampede starts in a couple of days. We can go to the rodeo, and there's always lots of parties. I can show you off.' He grinned across the table at her.

'You mean you want me to come for several days?' Merle asked slowly, starting to feel uneasy.

Leon shrugged. 'Days, weeks, I don't know, darling. I hope for a long time. We're good together, Merle. I want you to live with me.'

Slowly Merle extracted her hand from his. She felt a strange little ache near her heart, something like disappointment. An ugly suspicion was growing inside her, filling her with cold dread. 'Leon, is that why you made love to me this morning?'

His eyes narrowed, his smile faded. 'What are you getting at?'

She took a deep shuddering breath. 'I want to know if you made love to me this morning so you could convince me to go with you to Calgary?' Deny it, Leon, please deny it, she silently pleaded.

'And why would I want to do that?' he asked in a deadly cold voice, his face taking on a greyish tinge.

'I can't scout your well if I'm in Calgary, can I?'

Her voice quivered and she cleared her throat. 'You said you hoped for a long time. Just how long would that be, Leon?' He didn't comment and she forced the next words out. 'Until the well's in? Is that how long, Leon?'

His eyes were like hard green jewels set in a wooden mask. Merle dropped her gaze to his hand resting on the table, staring at it as he clenched it into a hard fist, the knuckles white. The seconds ticked by slowly as she waited for him to answer her, the tension building to screaming pitch.

'Are you suggesting that I would ... *prostitute* myself to get you off this well?' he finally said, his tone somehow more menacing because he spoke so softly.

Put like that it sounded so incredibly sordid. Merle kept her eyes lowered, chewing her lower lip. She hadn't meant it quite that way, but she *would* have to give up her job if she went with him. 'I didn't say that the only reason you ... we ... you have to admit that you've pulled some pretty rotten tricks to get me off this project.'

'And what happened this morning was another "rotten trick"?'

'That's what I'm asking you,' she whispered miserably.

'Perhaps I should be asking you the same question,' he said harshly. 'I just assumed you weren't sleeping with Larson, but I don't know that, do I? Is that how you operate?' Angry colour was starting to build along his cheekbones but there was still an unnatural whiteness about his mouth. 'Damn you—you must have been disappointed when you got nothing from me,' Leon jeered. 'What were you hoping for? That I would whisper pressure readings and core reports in your ear instead of endearments?' His gaze swept the room. 'Or have you been ransacking this room while I was in the shower washing the scent of you off me? Too bad my briefcase was in the other room and locked, isn't it, Merle?'

Merle's breathing was ragged as she looked up at him. Why hadn't she kept her suspicions to herself? She could tell by his reaction that they were unfounded. She could sense the hurt beneath his anger. 'I'm sorry, Leon. I—I was wrong . . . I know you didn't——'

'So now that I start questioning *your* motives you back off,' he interrupted. His anger was gaining momentum, burning out everything but the desire to hit back. 'But it's too late, Merle. You've shown me that you don't care about *anything* but that well and what's going on out there. You live in a pig sty rather than spend two minutes away from your spying to clean it up. You're obsessed with your sordid little job. You'd give your life, your health to find out about that well—why should your body be any different?' He laughed suddenly, a harsh, ugly sound that made Merle flinch. 'This morning . . . I thought we made *love*, but that wasn't what you were doing at all. How appalled you must have been when you found out I wanted you to come live with me—a hooker with a client she can't get rid of.'

'Leon, no, please, you have to . . .'

'Have to what? Pay up now?' he interrupted cruelly. 'Are you presenting me with a bill?' He paused, his eyes raking over her in contemptuous inspection. Merle felt bile rise in her throat. Leon stood up abruptly and his chair crashed to the floor. He leaned across the table threateningly, his eyes shards of green glass. Merle felt the blood drain from her face. Her heart thundered in her chest as fear gripped her.

Slowly, he reached into the inner pocket of his suit jacket and pulled out his wallet. Carefully, he extracted five one-hundred dollar bills and held them out to her. 'Here, sorry it's not in the currency you wanted.'

Merle stared at the money, feeling sick inside. Wordlessly, she stood up to leave the room. Leon caught her by the wrist as she was skirting the table. 'Take it, Merle,' he bit out between clenched teeth.

'No!' Merle wrenched her arm to break his hold and he tightened his grip.

'Take the money, Merle. I would hate to think you sacrificed yourself this morning for nothing. You can buy yourself a new nightie,' he twisted her wrist viciously and she cried out. 'I'll break it, Merle. Take the money.'

Merle raised fearful eyes to his face. Leon wasn't teasing her now, he meant it. His fingers tightened on her arm and she gasped, 'I'll take it.'

Leon dropped her arm and shoved the money into her uninjured hand. 'Get out, Merle.' He was breathing heavily, his face flushed with anger as he put a hand into his pocket. Pulling out the two sets of keys to her Blazer, he tossed them on to the table in front of her. 'Get out of here, Merle. You want information on my well, you'll just have to go back up on your hill.'

'Leon . . .?' Merle pleaded. How could she have been so foolish? She could have just said no . . . or yes. Yes . . . yes, she wanted to live with him. She hadn't just fallen for him; it wasn't simple infatuation. She loved him, must have loved him for a long time. All she wanted was Leon, to be with him for however long he wanted her. She didn't care about the well any more.

'Merle, get out. Now!' He turned his back on her, no longer able to bear the sight of her.

Merle bit her lip and picked up the keys. Slowly, she walked out of the unit. In the hall, she stopped, staring down at the wad of bills in her hand and feeling cold. Only now was the blood starting to return to the arm he had so brutally mistreated. It throbbed with the pain of bruised muscles, yet that pain was nothing compared to the heart-wound the money inflicted. Looking up, Merle realised she was by the vending machines. A large, cylindrical waste container stood next to the candy machine. Merle walked to it. Raising her hand, she uncurled the fingers that were wrapped around the money, letting the notes drift into the basket. Turning, Merle slowly walked to her room.

The jet was high overhead, a tiny dot in the broad blue sky leaving a wide white band behind it. The drone of its engines reached her ears, mingling with the rustle of summer-dried grasses, the steady throb of the drilling rig in the background. Merle followed its path with tear-filled eyes.

When would it end? When would the raw pain ease to a throbbing ache? How could she know? Always before, she had been the one to call it off, the one to walk away unscarred. When she had broken with Paul, she had only felt relief, her heart had not even been bruised. Now, it held a great gaping wound that filled her being with pain.

She had even called her mother, painfully aware that even though their relationship was flawed, she had no one else to turn to. Her friends of childhood had dropped away over the years, and she had never bothered to replace them. Ironically, Leon had probably come closer to being her friend than anyone else in recent years.

Her mother hadn't been home when she called, the message on her answering machine informing Merle that she was taking a Caribbean cruise but was due back soon. Would she meet someone? A man to be husband number four? Would he be the one who could finally fill Jake's shoes? Merle hoped so, for her mother, for herself. It would be easier knowing that someday she might find what she could have had with Leon with someone else.

Merle rolled on to her stomach, glancing un-interestedly at the drilling site a half-mile distant. She had come to the hilltop this afternoon after trying to reach her mother. Conscientiously, she noted the activities she observed in her little notebook, but knew she was not scouting the well. She made no attempt to collate the facts, to read into them the results of the drilling.

She studied her arm, tracing the bruises with her finger. Her wrist was blue-black and she could not move it without pain. It was physical evidence of Leon's opinion of her, should she be tempted to forget. He despised her, maybe hated her, and nothing she could do would take them back to this morning when she had been so happily preparing their breakfast. Merle rotated her wrist, finding the physical pain somehow comforting, as though it could somehow distract from the pain of bleeding emotions.

'Stop it!' She spoke aloud as tears pricked her eyes, startling a hare that had approached her still figure. The animal bounded away as Merle picked up her binoculars again and trained them on the site. She could not allow herself to wallow in self-pity. It had cost her Leon but the job was the only thing she had left. It was time she started doing it!

Over the next few days, she tried very hard to do that, forcing her thoughts away from Leon. Although he stayed in Calgary, it wasn't easy, for she could still feel his influence. He hadn't forgotten she was scouting the well and the rig workers launched a subtle campaign of harassment that made that only too clear.

It started one morning when she left her motel unit and found that someone had let the air out of all four tyres on the Blazer. It had taken her most of the day to locate a garage with a portable compressor who would come out to pump them back up. A few days later, she returned to the vehicle from her position on the hill and found that in her absence someone had broken in and scattered her camping equipment all over the prairie. When the truck refused to start the day following this incident, she wasn't surprised to discover that the rotor was missing.

Far worse than the vandalism of the truck was the personal persecution. She found herself being forced to drive further and further afield for her meals as she could no longer stand to eat at the truckstop. If any of the employees of Puma Resources were present when she was, they sent her leering looks, and made rude, over-loud comments as she passed their table. Twice, she was accosted in the parking lot as she was going to her truck. Though she wasn't harmed in anyway, the approaches had been insulting and vaguely threatening.

Perhaps the incidents though, were the answer to her anguish. Slowly, resentment started to build. She still couldn't think of Leon without pain, but the pain was gradually being overlaid by a veneer of anger.

Enemies . . . when she had told Leon that they were enemies she had never conceived just what the term could entail.

She arrived back at the motel late one evening, feeling tired and dispirited. She had had dinner at a small café some twenty miles distant, a meal which confirmed the diner's reputation as a 'greasy spoon'. While she had never considered the truckstop a particularly great place to eat, she was beginning to discover it was far better than most of the other restaurants in the area.

The room was in darkness when she let herself in and she switched on the overhead light. Looking around, she wondered what Leon would say if he saw it now. His criticism that she lived in a pig sty had gone home and she had cleared away the clutter and made a determined effort to keep it clean since then. It hadn't been as difficult as she had assumed it would be. Yet, as her eyes moved around the room, she felt lonely and a little lost. The room looked much as it had the first day she had moved in. When it had been a mess, at least it had been *her* mess, but now, it looked like just what it was: a cold, impersonal motel room.

Sighing unhappily, Merle pulled off her shirt and jeans, and carefully folding them away, went into the bathroom to have her bath. Hopefully, the well would come in soon. All summer there had been strong indications that they were finding natural gas. This afternoon she had heard the rumble of gas rising in the drill pipe. A short time later, the geologist had gone out to the foreman and they had started to pull out the stem. She had left when it became obvious they were going to take a core sample. They probably wouldn't be finished getting the sample until morning and she wanted to be there when it came out. If it was encouraging, she knew they would do a drill stem test. This procedure was carried out by lowering a perforated pipe attached to the hollow drill stem into the hole and releasing the reservoir of gas and fluids into it. Gauges placed inside the pipe measured the reservoir pressures and flow capacity. If the results were acceptable, the drilling could stop there and Puma Resources would have a gas well.

Merle relaxed back into the warm water, closing her eyes momentarily. She hoped Leon would decide to settle on the gas well so the job would be over. From the indications she had, it would be a good well. On the other hand, they might decide to go for broke and drill deeper in hopes of finding oil. That would mean the job could take several more weeks.

Realising she was starting to doze off, Merle got out of the tub and wrapped a towel around herself. Her hair was slightly damp from the steam and listlessly she began combing out the tangles. It had grown a lot over the summer and she knew she should have it cut. On the other hand, maybe she wouldn't, she thought, brushing it away from her face. She kept it short because it was easier to take care of when she was working, especially if she was camping in the bush. Maybe she wouldn't take another scouting job when she finished this one.

The hand holding the brush froze. Though she had occasionally entertained doubts, felt discouraged about her job, this was the first time she had ever seriously considered quitting. As the idea grew, she knew that was what she wanted to do. She was tired of the loneliness, the long hours of boredom which no longer seemed rewarded when she gathered some clue.

Her thoughts went to Greg Larson, the way she had let him kiss her, caress her. She hadn't even liked him, but because she needed the information he had, she had actually encouraged him. Had he really fallen in love with her? Merle shuddered as her thoughts veered to the question. She had been hurt by Leon, but it had been a hurt of her own making. Had Greg felt the same way she did—the tearing agony that was always beneath the surface? She turned away from the mirror, unable to bear her own image. Was she so despicable that she had deliberately put someone through what she had been going through since Leon had sent her away? And would she continue scouting and do the same thing again with another man and another well?

But how could she quit? What would she do? She disliked secretarial work, which was the only other job skill she had. 'You could get married.' She knew that would be her mother's advice. There were a couple of men other than Jack Franklin that she dated when she was in Calgary and she knew that with encouragement, she could extract a proposal from either of them. But was that what she wanted? Would she really marry someone she didn't love? She couldn't do it when she was twenty and engaged to Paul, could she now simply because she didn't know what else to do with her life? And if she did, would that be any different than leading Greg Larson on?

Slowly, she resumed brushing her hair. She remembered how she had felt that morning when she was cooking breakfast for Leon. It had felt like being married to him—and she had been very happy that morning. She had acknowledged that she loved him, but until now she had never thought beyond having an affair with him. Marriage to Leon—she had always viewed marriage as a form of woman's bondage, of being chained to a man by a bit of legal paper. But what of loving and sharing and giving? Marriage to Leon would be that. Perhaps a marriage licence was merely the final link in the chain of love that bound a man and woman.

Merle walked to the bed and pulled the covers back. Discarding the towel, she pulled on her nightgown and slipped between the sheets. As she turned restlessly beneath the bedclothes, she cursed once again her carelessness at misplacing her sleeping pills. She would need one tonight. It was going to be a lot harder than usual to keep the tears at bay. 'Days, weeks, a long time': those had been Leon's words. Leon hadn't wanted to complete that chain. If he had said 'forever' and forged that last link, she knew that she wouldn't be sleeping alone tonight in a motel room, somewhere off the No 1 Highway between Medicine Hat and Calgary.

When Merle arrived on the hilltop the next morning, the crew had just finished pulling out the core sample. The truck from the firm that supplied test equipment was parked near the office and Merle knew they would be examining the core here at the site and not sending it to Calgary.

She waited impatiently for them to finish the tests on the sample, wishing she were back in a busy office. At least there would have been people around instead of this infernal solitude. She didn't want to be alone with her thoughts. She felt she would have gladly typed a four-hundred page report just to keep her mind occupied. Leon, her job, her future: the problems tumbled around in her head all through the long, hot day. She couldn't even go back to the motel because she didn't know when or if they would do a drill stem test and she had to keep an eye on the site.

When the sun dipped to the horizon that afternoon, she still hadn't come to terms with her life. The geologist hadn't ordered a drill stem test and, when sundown approached, Merle knew he would probably wait until the next morning. As she started the walk back to the truck, all she had to show for her day was a painful throbbing behind her temples.

She was several hundred yards from the Blazer when she noticed a plume of dust rise a few feet in front of her. Frowning, Merle stopped walking and stared at the spot where the disturbance in the sand had occurred. Unable to fathom what it could have been, she was about to walk on when something whizzed past her cheek. She heard a splintering sound as it hit the branch of a tuft of sage brush behind her.

Someone was shooting at her!

She was dropping to the ground when the third bullet hit a nearby rock, shattering it. One of the fragments caught her on the cheek and she felt the stinging cut as she flattened herself to the ground. Merle lay rigid with fear as she waited for the next shot. She counted the seconds, wondering if each one would be her last. She was bleeding from the cut, but she ignored the warm liquid that was spilling down her cheek, turning the sand crimson.

She didn't know how long she lay there, centuries maybe, but she knew by the growing darkness that the sun had finally gone below the horizon. She waited several more minutes before moving. Finally, when it was almost completely dark, she eased herself off the ground and, running in a half crouch, made it to the Blazer. Her only thought was to get back to the motel, to the safety of her room.

She covered the seven miles to the motel in five minutes. Jamming on the brakes, she jerked the Blazer to a stop and jumped out, slamming the door behind her. She was about to dart into the motel when she saw Leon's red Blazer parked two spaces away from her truck. The shaft of pain that shot through her almost caused her to double over. Until this moment her mind had been too numbed by panic to consider who had fired the shots. Did he hate her this much? Wave after wave of anguish washed through her, undermining further the thin edge she had retained on her sanity. How would she bear this final blow? How could she live knowing he hated her enough to try to kill her?

She stumbled into the motel, tears blinding her. *He hated her enough to kill her*. The words ricocheted around her mind over and over again. She reached the door to her room and fumbled the key out of her pocket. Her hands were shaking as she tried to insert it into the lock and she dropped it. Merle leaned weakly against the door, trying to gain enough composure to reach down and pick it up.

Merle heard footfalls approaching along the hall and kept her face turned to the door. An involuntary tremor passed through her. How could he have done this to her? The footsteps halted behind her. Merle stiffened her spine, resolutely keeping her back to the corridor. She couldn't bear to face anyone, to talk to anyone right now.

'What's wrong?' Leon demanded with harsh impatience.

She didn't turn around. 'Go away,' she whispered, huskily. She felt the fragile hold she retained on her control starting to slip. The key to her room still lay at her feet and she reached down to pick it up, clutching the doorknob for support.

Leon clasped her shoulder when she had straightened and was trying to fit the key into the lock. 'What's wrong?' he reiterated, his tone softened with reluctant concern.

Merle jerked away from him. His touch was like a hammerblow on her already shattered nerves, and she spun around, screaming, 'You *know* what's wrong! You did this to me!'

The blood drained from Leon's face when he saw hers. Tears were streaming from her eyes, mingling with the caked blood from the gash on her cheek. 'Oh my God!' He saw her sway and his arms went out to catch her.

She cringed away, flattening herself against the door, her eyes dilating. 'No, don't come near me,' she ordered, her voice tinged with panic. She eyed him warily and Leon could read the fear in her eyes. 'Don't hurt me.'

'What happened?' he asked urgently. She stared at him mutely, the rise and fall of her breasts uneven. 'Please, Merle, I'm not going to hurt you, but you have to tell me what happened to you,' he coaxed, forcing a gentler tone.

'You know,' she muttered, wrapping her arms around her. She lowered her head, feeling suddenly cold and empty. 'I knew you were angry with me,' she said bitterly, 'but I didn't think you would do anything like this. I thought . . . I didn't know you hated me that much.'

Leon heard a door open, followed by laughter as a couple entered the hallway. 'Merle, we can't talk here. Let me have your key and we'll talk in your room.'

Merle shook her head, her fingers tightening on the key. 'No, I don't want to talk to you. Leave me alone, just leave me alone. You've done enough to me.' She turned her back on him, and tried once again to open her door. Finally, her shaking fingers managed to insert the key into the lock and she turned the knob.

Leon was right behind her as she slipped through the opening. She tried to force the door closed behind her, shutting him out, but he propelled it inward and forced his way inside.

Angrily, Merle faced him as he slammed the door behind them. 'Get out of here! I told you to leave me alone.'

'Not until I find out what happened. Somehow you seem to think I'm responsible, so I at least have a right to know what I'm supposed to have done.' His own temper was rising, and anger chiselled his features into harsh lines.

'You know damn well what you've done,' Merle retorted. The tears had started again and she brushed them away impatiently. When they continued to flow she turned her back on him. She dug her nails into her palms, trying to stop the silent scream that was echoing in her head from breaking free. 'Leon, just get out of here,' she pleaded unsteadily, her anger dissolving with her composure. 'I know you despise me, hate me, but have a little mercy. I'm not going to tell anyone what happened if that's what you're worried about. So, please, just leave me alone.'

He came up behind her and touched her arm. She flinched away from him as though she had been burnt. A sob rose in her throat and her shoulders shook as she suppressed it. She heard Leon mutter something but couldn't make out what it was because the blood was roaring in her ears. She was losing the battle to control the emotions churning through her and knew at any moment she would break. At last, she sensed him move away, then heard the slam of the door closing behind him.

CHAPTER EIGHT

A FEW minutes later, Merle lay huddled on the bed, her shoulders shaking with sobs, her face buried in a pillow. She didn't hear the door to her room open, didn't hear the man go into the bathroom and run the tap. Only when she felt the edge of the bed depress and Leon's hand on her shoulder, gently turning her, did she realise he had returned.

She stared up into his face, bewildered, her eyes drenched with tears. Putting his arm around her, he helped her to sit up and pressed a glass of water into her hand. He reached into his shirt pocket and pulled out a vial of capsules. Opening it, he shook out one of the small red tablets and put it into her free hand. 'I want you to take this, Merle. You're overwrought; it will calm you down.'

She looked from the pill resting in her palm, to the bottle, recognising her sleeping pills. They must have been in the bathroom all along. How did he always know where her things were when she didn't even know herself?

'Merle, please,' Leon said gently, taking the capsule from her and holding it to her lips. 'Take the pill. Then, I'm going to clean up your cheek for you, okay?'

Bemused, she allowed Leon to place it in her mouth, then took a sip from the glass of water to wash it down. Leon took the glass from her and set it on the bedside table. He picked up the first-aid kit he had placed there earlier and opened it. Taking out a bottle of antiseptic, he poured some on to a wad of cotton and started wiping the blood from the gash on her cheek.

Merle continued to stare at him, noting the grim concentration on his face as he carefully tended the cut. When it was cleaned, he took a plaster from the kit and covered the gash. The task completed, he smiled stiffly at her. 'It doesn't look too bad. It should heal in a few days and I don't think it will scar.'

He stood up and started replacing the supplies in the first-aid kit. 'Why are you doing this, Leon?' Merle asked.

He didn't reply, but continued filling the kit. When he had finished, he snapped it shut, then turned to face her. The pill was doing its work. Her eyes no longer held that wild look they had earlier and the trembling had stopped. 'Merle,' he said firmly, 'I know you insist I know what happened, but I don't. Now that you've calmed down a little, do you think you can tell me what got you into this state?'

Merle stared down at the bedspread, her fingertip tracing the pattern of the quilting. 'One of your men shot at me,' she answered quietly, then looked up at him, her eyes dark and accusing. 'They wouldn't do that unless you told them to.'

He studied her face with narrowed eyes, his own face pale under his tan. 'Tell me exactly what happened out there this afternoon.'

In a remote, unemotional tone, she related what had happened after she left her position on the hill that afternoon. The sleeping pill was taking hold of her now, and her words began to slur as she talked. Finally, she reached the end of the story and yawned.

'Go away, Leon. I want to sleep now. You don't have to pretend your innocence any more.' She curled up on the bed, putting her back to him. Within seconds she was asleep.

'What the hell are you doing in my room?'

Leon jerked awake. Merle was sitting in the bed, the blankets pulled up under her armpits, covering her breasts. She looked very young, with her hair tousled from sleep, her colour high. Her eyes, though, looked like a pair of steel daggers and from her expression, he was glad they weren't; she would have used them on him to cut him into shark bait.

He sat up straighter, flexing the muscles in his back and rubbing the stiffness that had settled in his neck after spending most of the night in the chair.

'I asked what you're doing in my room? I suggest you get out before I change my mind about calling the cops.' This was starting to become a habit: waking up and finding Leon. At least, *this* time he wasn't in the bed. She swallowed hard, wishing he didn't look quite so disturbingly attractive in the morning light. His light brown hair was ruffled as though he had combed his hand through it. He was wearing a pale yellow sports shirt, open at the neck, the sleeves rolled to the elbow to expose tanned forearms. His slacks were faintly crumpled, though the material stretched taut over his hard, muscled thighs as he shifted in the chair.

Her heart gave a little jerk as the memory of his lovemaking flashed through her mind, his nude body pressed against her. Her eyes drifted to his mouth, the finely chiselled upper lip, the lower lip, full and sensuous. She knew his kiss, the mobile pressure of that mouth on hers. Her pulse quickened and her tongue came out to moisten dry lips. Appalled by what she was thinking, what she was wanting, she jerked her mind back to the present. For Lord's sake, Merle, he tried to *kill* you! She glared at him with renewed venom.

He was unable to suppress a smile as he took in her murderous stare. She reminded him of a little bantam hen getting ready to fly into a rage, her feathers ruffled and wings flapping.

She saw the twist of his lips and her own compressed in silent fury. Her robe was lying across the foot of the bed and Merle reached down and dragged it to her. Keeping the covers pulled up, she shrugged into it then jumped out of bed and stalked over to the phone. She was lifting the receiver when Leon said calmly, 'If you're calling the RCMP, I already have.' She turned to look at him and he smiled at her benignly. 'They should be here to talk to you in . . .' he glanced at his watch, '. . . about a half an hour.'

'*You* called the police?'

'Last night. You *did* say someone had shot at you?'

'Yes, but . . .?' Merle spread her hands in a bewildered gesture. He was the one who had shot at her, or at least, given the order. It didn't make any sense for him to have called the police.

'I didn't have anything to do with the shooting, Merle,' he answered the unspoken question. 'I went out with the police last night to question the men at the well. It doesn't look like any of them are responsible for the shooting, either. You left the hill a few minutes before sundown and the shots were fired while you were on the way to your truck. Is that right?'

Merle nodded.

'Most of the men were on the site at the time because of the core testing. The ones who weren't can all account for their whereabouts and they weren't anywhere near the hill.'

'And where were you?' Merle demanded. Who would want to shoot at her if it wasn't Leon or the rig workers?

'I drove down from Calgary yesterday afternoon. I reached the motel about a half an hour before sunset and went for a swim. I was only just going out to the site when I saw you,' he explained patiently.

'I don't understand.' She shook her head in a confused motion.

'Whoever took those shots at you had nothing to do with Puma Resources, Merle. You'll just have to trust me on that.'

'Trust you?' she cried, struggling to hang on to her indignation. 'After all you've done to me this summer, you expect me to trust you?' Though the question was delivered in a cutting tone, that hard, cold ball of misery that had resided in the pit of her stomach ever since last night was slowly starting to thaw. She could handle the shooting. After all, she was an oil scout and sometimes these things happened. Once, some workers from a site she had been scouting had chopped down the tree she was using as a vantage point while she was still in it. What she couldn't handle was knowing Leon, the man she was in love with, had wanted to have her killed.

He lowered his head, raking both hands through his hair. When he looked up again, his expression was impatient. 'Look, you know I was in a flaming temper when I threatened to break your arm. It was an . . . act of passion. But, damn it, Merle, there's a bloody big difference between that and a shooting done in cold blood.'

'And all the other things, I suppose they were "acts of passion"?'

'I'll admit I've tried to get you off the well, but

most of the things I've done have been ... practical jokes, not things that could hurt you. I never expected you to stay out all night when I poured the oil in the mud pit.' He smiled faintly at the memory and Merle's blood pressure rose.

'The harassment from your workers, the snide remarks, the crude passes everytime I go into the truckstop, those are practical jokes? You have a very bizarre sense of humour, Leon.'

'You brought that on yourself, Merle,' Leon said harshly. 'I told you what Larson had said about you at the site. I can't be blamed if my men see you as easy game.'

Merle glared at him, her lips pressed into a tight line. She couldn't find an answer for this so she said, defensively, 'And is my truck easy game, too?'

'Your truck?'

'Are you denying your men have been vandalising it on *your orders*?'

'Nobody touched your truck, Merle,' Leon denied, impatiently. 'My orders to the men were to leave you alone as long as you stayed up on the hill. If you started moving in closer, they were to let me know.'

'So it was just a coincidence that *all* the tyres went flat at once,' she stated acidly. 'And I imagine my camping equipment just hopped out of the back of it and threw itself all over the countryside.'

'That happened?' His brows drew together into a line.

'Yes. And one day, they stole the rotor from the distributor,' she added.

'I'll have a talk with the crew. Those were not my orders, Merle, and if any of them are responsible, I'll deal with them.' He looked at his watch. 'The police will be here shortly. You had better get dressed, they want you to show them where the shooting took place.'

'Now, Miss, you said you were here when you first realised someone was shooting at you. Is that correct?'

Merle looked at the young corporal impatiently. Was the man a complete idiot? How many times did she have to tell him what happened? She glanced over at Leon. She had been rather surprised that he had come with them, following behind the police car in his Blazer. She hoped that meant they wouldn't start doing the drill stem test at the site until he could be there.

'Yes, I was about here.'

'And you didn't hear the shots?'

Merle shook her head. 'I told you, I was walking back to my truck when I saw the sand lift over there.' She pointed to a spot about ten feet in front of her where a second officer was using a shovel trying to find the bullet. 'I didn't know what it was, so I stopped. The second bullet hit that bush behind me and that's when I realised someone was shooting at me, so I dove the for ground. As I was going down, a bullet hit a rock over there and a fragment hit me in the cheek.' She automatically touched the plaster on her face, her eyes seeking Leon. She wished she could understand him. It seemed so strange that he should have helped her last night and this morning when it was apparent that he was still angry with her.

'It's strange you didn't hear the shots,' the officer commented.

'I had a lot on my mind, so I guess that's why I didn't hear them.'

He looked at her doubtfully, then shrugged. These

oil scouts were a damned nuisance and it wouldn't bother him if they shot the lot of them. Twice in the last year he had been called out in the middle of the night to investigate break-ins at drilling sites. He knew scouts were responsible, but the culprits had been too clever to get caught.

'Well, Miss, I'll talk to the ranchers in the area and see if they saw anyone. It was probably a hunter. The light is pretty uncertain at that time of day and some of them will shoot at anything that moves.'

'Do you think you'll find out who did it?' Leon spoke for the first time since they had come out here.

'Probably not,' the corporal admitted. 'If it was a hunter, he would have been shooting out of season and isn't likely to come forward.'

The second officer came over to them and handed the corporal the spent bullet he had retrieved from the sand. From the expression in his face as he studied it, Merle got the impression that until now he hadn't even believed she had been shot at.

'Couldn't you locate the gun from that bullet?' Leon asked.

The officer laughed. 'You watch too much television. This is from a 30-30. Do you have any idea how many rifles of that gauge are in this country? Every rancher between Medicine Hat and Calgary probably owns at least one. And then you have all the hunters who live in town and just hunt on the weekends. You'd never locate the gun that this was fired from if you looked for a year.'

'So that's it?' Leon asked, disbelieving. 'You're just going to forget it?'

'I said we'll ask around. There's not much else we can do.' He turned to Merle. 'We'll drive you back to the motel now, Miss.'

'I'll take Miss Halliday back,' Leon interposed firmly.

The corporal looked at her and Merle shrugged. He motioned to the other officer and they walked away to their car.

Merle waited until the police car had driven off before turning her attention to Leon. He was staring at the spot where the officer had found the bullet, a brooding expression on his face. Finally, he looked over to her and motioned her to accompany him down the hill.

'Merle,' Leon said as they were walking to his Blazer, 'I want you to stay away from the hill for a while.'

'Why?' She stopped, turning to look at him, her expression faintly defiant.

'At least give the police a few days to see if they can find out who did the shooting.'

'You heard what they said. It was a hunter; they'll probably never find out who shot at me.'

She started to move on and he stopped her by placing his hand on her arm. 'Don't you think it's odd that you didn't hear the shots?'

'No, I don't. I told you, I had a lot on my mind at the time.' Like you, she added silently.

'Maybe that would explain why you didn't hear the first shot, but what about the others? Why didn't you hear those? Merle, you're an oil scout, you can't have been that unobservant.'

'Well, I guess I wasn't being very observant last night, was I?'

'Or, whoever did it used a silencer.'

She gave him a derisory look. 'The officer was right, Leon. You *do* watch too much television.' She wished he would shut up. The explanation that the shots were from a careless hunter suited her fine. She didn't want to consider any other possibilities, they would only make her nervous about coming back out to the hill.

'Merle, it wouldn't hurt to be a little cautious over the next few days. Take some time off, enjoy the last of the good summer weather. At least, give them a chance to check things out, okay?'

'It wouldn't hurt, Leon?' Merle asked archly. 'Look, I know you're doing a drill stem test sometime today. Is all this talk a delaying tactic so I miss it?'

He gave her an exasperated look and she walked on. She climbed in the passenger door of the Blazer and settled back in the seat, her arms crossed, to wait for him. He joined her in a moment, though he didn't start the truck. Instead, he turned in his seat and studied her. 'Okay, Merle. You win this round. If you know there's a test, you must know it will take us a few days to decide whether we're going on or whether we'll settle for a gas well. Will you promise me that you'll stay off the hill until the police have a chance to finish their investigation, if I promise to let you know which way we're going to go as soon as it's decided?'

She cast him a suspicious look. 'How do I know you're not trying to trick me, again?'

'You don't,' Leon said tiredly. 'But I don't break my word, and I don't want you up on that hill by yourself until this is cleared up.'

Merle stared at him thoughtfully, biting her lower lip in indecision. Leon acted as if he really were worried about her. But it had to have been an accident. Nobody would shoot at her deliberately, unless it was to stop her scouting the well, and she had to admit, she did believe him when he said he had nothing to do with it.

'Come on, Merle. Think of it as a little holiday,' Leon persisted.

'I must be an absolute fool to trust you,' Merle said, disgustedly, turning to look out the window.

'But you promise?'

'I promise,' she muttered.

In the truckstop that evening, Merle toyed with her lettuce, covertly watching the man seated across from her. She wondered why he had offered to eat with her if he wasn't even going to talk to her. After last night and this morning, she thought maybe he had got over being angry with her, but obviously he hadn't.

Leon finished his own salad, and pushing aside the empty plate, sat back to wait for the waitress to bring the main course. 'I'm heading back to Calgary in the morning,' he said. 'You might want to do the same. I can get in touch with you there if we decide to go in with the drilling.' God, his voice was cold! She almost wished he had continued with the silent treatment.

'I'll stay around the motel,' Merle replied moodily, shoving her own plate aside. She knew if she was in Calgary, she would have to check in with her boss, Frank Destry, and she didn't want to. She hadn't told Wild Rose about the gas yet, and for some reason she wanted to put it off. Besides, how could she explain the bargain she had made with Leon this morning? Frank wouldn't expect her to continue the job if she really were in danger, but he would undoubtedly agree with her and the police that the shots had come from a careless hunter.

Before Leon could comment, Sally arrived at the table with their meal. The ice left his eyes like a spring thaw in the St Lawrence as he turned his attention to the waitress.

Having delivered their plates, Sally hovered over Leon. Would he like ketchup? Was his steak rare enough? Did he want more coffee? When she finally walked off, Merle couldn't help saying, 'Why didn't you ask her to cut your meat for you? I'm sure she wouldn't have minded.'

'I'm sure she would,' Leon said coldly, his features resuming their frozen lines. 'She does her job—but she isn't obsessed by it.' He concentrated on his meal as Merle stared at him in frustration for several seconds.

Finally, she blurted out, 'Just what do you want me to do? Tear up my report for Wild Rose and forget the whole thing?'

Carefully, Leon set down his knife and fork and met her gaze. 'Since it's pretty obvious to me that that report is the most important thing in your life I could hardly expect you to destroy it. What I do want is for you to avoid getting yourself killed while scouting my well. I don't want that kind of scandal connected with a project of mine.' He picked up his silverware and resumed his meal, dismissing her.

So that's why he's so concerned about me, Merle thought, pretending an appetite for her own dinner that she didn't feel. Instead of angering her, the knowledge only added to her depression. *He* was the most important thing in her life, not the job or the report, but how would she ever make him understand? She had no experience at being honest with a man. Before Leon, she had considered herself something of an expert when it came to handling men. She knew how to string them along, play on their emotions, get whatever she wanted from them. She peeked at Leon through her lashes. He had seen through all the games she played—only he couldn't see that she wasn't trying to play games with him any more.

Merle remained silent through the rest of the meal,

lost in thought. If Leon really was the most important thing in her life, how could she betray him and her love for him by helping his rivals? With his assertion that it was the most important thing in her life, every time she thought about handing in her report, she felt guilty. When she had asked Leon if he wanted her to tear up her report, she hadn't been serious, but she wondered if maybe that wasn't what she should do. It wouldn't change his feelings for her, but didn't she owe him a certain amount of loyalty because she loved him?

On the drive back to the motel, Merle was still preoccupied and in consequence, didn't notice they had arrived until Leon had parked the Blazer and turned off the engine.

'You've been awfully quiet.' He shifted in his seat so he could look at her. 'I hope you're not trying to figure out some way of getting out of your promise.'

'I'm not,' Merle said, then added, 'though I do think you're over-reacting.'

He let that pass, saying, instead, 'Are you sure you don't want to go back to Calgary for a few days? I'm sure your mother would like to see you if you haven't been back all summer.'

'I'm sure she would,' Merle agreed drily. 'However, as I don't particularly want to see her, I'll just stay here.' She could just imagine Edith's reaction if she found out she had been shot at. It would provide one more weapon in her arsenal of reasons why Merle should quit oil scouting.

'Well, as a matter of fact, I called her last night and . . .'

'You did *what*?' Merle exclaimed, outraged.

'I said I called her,' Leon repeated firmly. 'I felt she had a right to know what had happened. She thought it would be wise for you to stay with her until the police have finished their investigation. She suggested I could give you a lift into Calgary with me tomorrow and I agreed.'

At his last sentence, Merle's anger started to slip. She had never forgotten the expression in Jack Franklin's face that night they had met her mother in the restaurant, the mixture of embarrassment and horror as her mother began prying into his life, her motive obvious. Suddenly, Merle had a picture of that awful black dog Leon had had the rancher scare her off his property with, her mother's head superimposed on its body. She could see it slowly advancing on Leon. Helpless to banish the image, Merle started to laugh.

Leon was staring at her as though she had suddenly lost her mind. 'Oh, Leon,' Merle finally managed to say. 'Did you tell her who you were?'

'Of course.'

At that, Merle laughed even harder, holding her ribs when they started to ache. Edith would be far worse with Leon than Jack because she would undoubtedly recognise his name. By now, three-quarters of Calgary would know that Merle knew the oil tycoon, Leon Crane—and if she knew anything at all about her mother, most of them would have the impression that the wedding invitations were in the mail.

Wiping tears of mirth from her eyes, Merle looked over to Leon. 'You have no idea what you've done, have you?' He merely frowned at her. 'My mother . . .' Merle started to giggle again. 'She probably booked the church on the strength of that one phone call. Unless you fancy being forced into marriage with me, I think you'd just better forget all about taking me to my mother's.'

Leon gave her the strangest look, and instantly all her amusement vanished. Hastily, Merle averted her head, reaching for the door handle. Even all her mother's machinations could never succeed in making Leon want her for his wife. How could such a feeling of desolation replace what moments ago had been laughter? She had to blink rapidly to hold back tears. Opening the door, Merle scrambled out of the Blazer. Keeping her face turned slightly away from Leon, she said, 'I'm staying at the motel. Don't worry, I won't break my promise.' Then, because she didn't want him to guess how she was feeling, she added harshly, 'And don't forget *yours*.' Without waiting for him to comment, she ran into the motel.

Merle sat watching the two boys who were playing in the shallow end of the pool, wishing she wasn't so bored and didn't have to work so hard at not thinking about Leon. She hadn't seen him for over a week, he hadn't even said goodbye before leaving for Calgary. She had had an uncomfortable telephone conversation with her mother the morning he left. As she had suspected, her mother wasn't the least concerned about the shooting. She was far more interested in how Merle happened to know Leon Crane and just what their relationship was. In the end, Merle had finally told her to mind her own business and had slammed down the receiver.

The children were playing with a large orange beach ball, and Merle focused her attention on them, shutting her mind to other thoughts. They were taking turns sitting on the ball, trying to sink it, but they were too small to have much success. Her knowledge of children wouldn't fill a decent-sized paragraph, but she thought they couldn't be more than five or six years old, even though they appeared to be good swimmers.

Finally, they combined efforts and managed to push the ball right to the bottom of the pool. When they released it, it shot out of the water and rolled a few feet from Merle. Laughing at their expressions of achievement, Merle got off her lounger and retrieved the ball for them.

'You want to come swimming with us?' the smaller of the two asked as she tossed the ball back into the water.

Merle hesitated. She hadn't had that in mind when she went after the ball. 'Please,' the other boy pleaded. 'Mom won't let us swim in the deep end without a grown-up.' He pointed to a woman sitting in a shaded lounger on the opposite side of the pool. Noticing her son's gesture, the woman struggled out of the lounger and walked over to Merle.

As she approached, Merle felt a twinge of pity for the woman. 'And I thought I was worn out after scouting all summer.' If this was what having kids did for you, Merle was glad she was never likely to become a mother. The woman couldn't have been much older than herself, yet her face was gaunt to the point of being haggard. Her complexion was pallid, her blue eyes dull and lifeless. Wisps of faded blonde hair escaped from an elastic at her nape and the cotton sundress she wore hung loosely over her frame.

'I hope they weren't bothering you,' the woman apologised.

Merle looked back at the boys. Even the woman's *voice* had been tired. 'Not at all. They just want me to swim with them.'

'Well, don't let them talk you into doing anything you don't want to do,' the woman warned, smiling.

'Oh, I don't mind. They said you didn't want them swimming in the deep end without an adult. I'd be happy to swim with them.'

'You're sure you wouldn't mind?' The woman's face softened as she looked at the boys. 'I would really appreciate it if you would. We were hoping to meet my husband in Calgary today, but I wasn't feeling well, so we stopped. They were disappointed about not seeing their dad so I told them they could use the pool. Unfortunately, I don't feel up to going in with them.'

'I don't mind.' Merle hesitated a fraction of a second, then continued, 'In fact, if you wanted to go lay down for a nap, I wouldn't mind looking after the kids for a couple of hours.' Now that she realised the woman was in ill-health, and not just worn out from looking after the boys, the idea of looking after them became attractive. 'I'll take good care of them. My name's Merle Halliday, you can ask them about me at the desk. I've been staying here for several weeks.'

'I'm sure I could trust you. It's not that, I just don't want to impose.'

'It wouldn't be an imposition. I'd enjoy it,' Merle assured her, hoping she was telling the truth. Somehow, she had missed out on the normal teenage experiences of babysitting, but looking down at the two boys, she thought it might be fun to take care of them for a few hours. It would give her something to do. Now that she was getting back to normal, physically and mentally, she was starting to get bored.

'Well,' the woman said doubtfully, 'if you really wouldn't mind. To tell you the truth, I do feel a little rough.'

'Don't worry about them. We'll have fun,' Merle

assured her, any doubts she might have entertained being lost in a surge of sympathy for the woman.

'Well then, thank you.' The woman smiled as she accepted. 'I guess I should introduce us. My name is Mary Blake, and this is Andrew and Sean.' She indicated the boys. 'Lisa's sleeping over there in her car bed. I doubt if she'll wake up for a couple of hours, but I'm in room fifteen if she does. You can send one of the boys in to get me.'

Merle's smile wavered slightly as she glanced over at the car bed. She hadn't realised the woman had a baby. If what she knew about children wouldn't fill a paragraph, what she knew about babies wouldn't take up a sentence. Well, maybe it wouldn't wake up. Mary Blake could be damned sure that if it did one of the boys would be in to get her mighty fast.

Fortunately, Mary Blake didn't seem to notice Merle's doubt about her ability to care for a baby and left the pool area a couple of minutes later with an easy mind.

For the next half hour, Merle dived and splashed in the pool with the boys. She didn't think Mary needed to have any doubts about their swimming ability, as she found she was easily out-classed by them even though she had been doing a lot of swimming over the summer. Their expertise amazed her as Andrew, the larger of the two, confided he was only six. He told her he would be starting grade one in Calgary when they got there and seemed to consider six to be considerably older than she did, much to Merle's amusement. Sean, the smaller boy, was five, and even more forthcoming than his older brother. *He* would be in kindergarten and was going to be a cowboy now that they were moving to Calgary. His father had promised him a pair of boots, and they would be new ones, he assured Merle, not hand-me-downs from his brother.

Merle had not gone to have a look at little Lisa yet, though she kept her ear tuned for a sound from her. She was half-afraid to look. If the baby did need something, Merle wouldn't have a clue how to handle it. She would hate to disturb Mary over something minor, so she decided to let sleeping dogs, or in this case babies, lie.

By the end of the half hour, Merle was worn out and she pulled herself up on to the concrete apron that surrounded the pool and lay in the sun to dry. The boys joined her almost immediately and they chattered to her, displaying typical sibling rivalry by trying to outshout one another to hold her attention. Nonetheless, she did learn something about their background. Their father had recently taken a job in Calgary and they were coming from Ontario now to join him. When they explained they hadn't been able to go with him initially because they were waiting for their baby sister to arrive, Merle paled slightly, her eyes going to the car bed. Just how *old* was that baby? She knew enough about babies to know she hoped it wasn't newborn.

She had just decided to stop being a coward and go have a look at the child when she saw the manageress of the motel come out to the pool area. Spotting Merle, the woman made a beeline for her, arriving faintly breathless.

'Miss Halliday?'

'Yes.'

'Oh, something terrible has happened,' she said, wringing her hands. 'Do you think I could speak to you in private for a moment?' She eyed the boys.

'Yes, of course,' Merle agreed, suggesting the boys

take their ball and play catch on the opposite side of
the pool. She had a strong sense of impending disaster
when she turned back to the woman.

'You're looking after Mrs Blake's children, aren't
you?'

Merle nodded slowly, her foreboding increasing
geometrically.

'She collapsed in the hall a little while ago. My
husband has taken her to the hospital in Medicine
Hat. I've tried to contact her husband, but I haven't
been able to reach him yet. You *will* be able to
continue with the children until we get things sorted
out, won't you?'

'Well . . .?' She looked at the car bed again. What
would she do when it woke up?

'Oh, please say you'll help. I really shouldn't even
be spending this time away frim the desk. This is
when everyone starts stopping for the night. If you
don't keep the children, I don't know what we'll do
with them.'

Put like that, what could she do but agree?

'Oh, thank you. You don't know how much I
appreciate this,' the manageress said gratefully. 'I'm
sure as soon as I reach Mr Blake he'll be able to
arrange something for tomorrow. Now, I must go.
Here's the key to Mrs Blake's room,' she said, handing
it to her. 'It will be easier for you to care for the
children in there.' As the woman scurried away, Merle
wondered how tomorrow could seem such a long time
away.

CHAPTER NINE

MERLE carried the car bed from the pool area with all the care of a man shifting a case of nitroglycerine. She would have gladly traded loads. She stopped briefly at her own room, changing from her bikini into jeans and a T-shirt, and filled up an overnight case with her night things and clothes for tomorrow, then shepherded the children to room fifteen. Once settled, Merle set about entertaining the boys, vainly hoping that the baby wouldn't awaken until morning. Fortunately, Mary Blake had left the boys well supplied with toys and games and Merle was able to keep them quiet by playing a board game with them.

Strangely enough, neither of the boys seemed overly concerned about their mother, seemingly content with Merle's explanation that she had had to go into the hospital for a few days. It wasn't until she overheard them whispering together later, speculating as to whether *this* time their mother would supply them with a baby brother, that she realised they didn't really understand that their mother was in fact ill. Merle didn't have the courage to correct their misapprehension.

The event she had been most dreading occurred when they had been in the room for about a half an hour. Lisa, to Merle's consternation, had turned out to be the smallest human being she had ever seen. By questioning the boys, Merle discovered she had been born only three weeks earlier and Merle wondered how fate could be so cruel to such a tiny baby as to place her in the care of such a rank amateur. As Merle stood gazing into the baby's calm, trusting blue eyes, she hoped she wasn't going to let her down.

With the help of Andrew and Sean, Merle found the carton of disposable nappies Mrs Blake had for Lisa, and changed her. She was rather surprised to find this task was relatively simple, partially because some of her nervousness disappeared when she discovered that the nappies fastened with tapes rather than pins so there was no danger of stabbing her charge. She wasn't even repulsed by the chore as she had feared she would be.

Her confidence increased when the baby accepted a bottle of formula quite readily, gulping it down while Merle cradled her in her lap. Lisa's brothers seemed to find Merle's inexperience extremely amusing but nevertheless eagerly pitched in to help, particularly with advice. Andrew prepared the formula, mixing it from a powdered concentrate and warm water, assuring Merle that his mother frequently allocated this job to him.

After draining the bottle, Lisa's eyelids fluttered down and Merle placed her back into the car bed, relieved that the baby seemed content to go back to sleep. The boys lost interest in the toy cars they had been racing across the carpeting while Merle fed the baby and wanted to watch television. As the request was made at the top of their lungs and the baby still didn't stir, Merle could see no harm in this and allowed them to turn on the set.

Everything is going swimmingly, Merle thought ten minutes later, even if the boys did insist the volume on the television be set at a level designed to wake the dead. As long as it didn't wake *Lisa*, Merle didn't mind.

Merle had settled herself in a chair while the boys sprawled on one of the beds and stared at the television screen. Room fifteen was larger than her own, being fitted with two double beds instead of the single queen size one, but other than that, there was little difference between the two. She read the back of the nappy carton, wishing Mrs Blake had had a book on child care. She had been forced to go through the woman's suitcase to find a clean sleeper for the baby, acutely conscious of a strong sense of trespassing. Removing all the baby's clothes, Merle had closed the case, expecting that Mr Blake would want to take it to his wife. She hoped Mary wasn't seriously ill and would be able to rejoin her children soon. Her illness could be connected to the recent childbirth, but once again, Merle was aware of her lack of knowledge in this area.

The cartoons the boys had been watching ended, and Andrew went over to the set and began flipping through the channels. Sean saw something he wanted to watch and demanded that his brother leave it on that show. This request resulted, naturally, in Andrew setting the dial on another station and the two boys started to quarrel. Merle had just decided to settle the argument by turning the set off altogether, when Lisa woke up and started to cry.

The first time the baby had awakened, she had only whimpered softly and had stopped as soon as Merle had picked her up. This time, however, the child was screaming when Merle reached the car bed, loud wails that didn't lessen when Merle lifted her out.

Merle cradled Lisa in her arms, murmuring softly to her, and wondering what could possibly be wrong. The baby's face was flushed with angry red, her features screwed up, as she took a deep breath in preparation for another scream.

'Andrew, maybe you had better fix her another bottle,' Merle told him, her voice raised to be heard over the racket in the room.

'But I want to watch this show,' the boy protested, holding his brother away from the set so he couldn't change the channel.

'Aunt Merle,' Sean wailed, 'can't we watch *Sesame Street*? I don't like police shows.'

'That show's for babies,' Andrew sneered at Sean.

'Boys, can't you see your sister is crying?' Merle snapped impatiently. 'Now, Andrew, will you do as you're told?'

'She's always crying. Mom just ignores her,' Andrew informed her, trying to wrestle his brother to the floor.

Merle thought this highly unlikely and once again ordered Andrew to prepare a bottle of formula. This time he obeyed, his expression sulky as he scuffled into the bathroom to mix the bottle with none of his former enthusiasm for helping. As his brother left the room, Sean shot him a triumphant look before switching the channel to the other station.

Merle paced the floor as she waited for Andrew to return with the bottle. The prolonged crying was starting to tire the baby, and her wails had deteriorated to heart-rending sobs which to Merle's mind were even worse. *If only she knew what was wrong*. She didn't really think Lisa was still hungry but had asked Andrew to fix another bottle because it was the only thing she could think of to do.

She turned at the window to make another circuit of the room, when the exterior door was pushed open. Leon stood in the doorway taking in the scene in one glance. Andrew emerged from the bathroom and rushed over to the television. Shoving his brother aside, he switched the station, nearly dropping the newly prepared bottle.

'I was looking for you,' Leon said loudly. 'I should have known I only needed to look for trouble and you'd be in the middle of it.' He strode into the room and going to the television, snapped it off. The boys started to protest and he silenced them with a look. Sweeping his eyes over the toys and game pieces littering the floor, he said, 'You two can clean this mess up while I see what Merle has done to the baby.'

He walked over to Merle and held out his arms to take the baby. 'I haven't *done* anything to the baby,' Merle protested, though she meekly relinquished her burden. 'I don't know what's wrong with her.'

Leon lifted the sobbing bundle to his shoulder and started stroking her back. 'Have you fed her?'

'Of course I have,' Merle answered shortly. '*And* I changed her, too,' she added when she saw him eyeing the carton of nappies. She could see those little lines at the corners of Leon's eyes starting to crinkle up. They always did that when he was laughing at her. Well, just let him take care of Lisa! He wouldn't find it nearly so funny then!

Leon thumped the baby firmly on her back and Merle made a grab for her. 'What are you doing?' she cried, outraged. 'Don't you dare hit her.'

'I'm not hitting her.' Leon stepped back out of range and administered another blow. 'I'm trying to get some of the gas out of her.' As he spoke, Lisa belched loudly and immediately stopped crying. Leon continued holding her, firmly running his hand up her back and the baby burped again.

'How did you know that was what was wrong with her?' Merle was staring at him in open-mouthed astonishment and he started to laugh.

'Since you won't believe I'm Superman, would you believe I'm really Mary Poppins?' Merle didn't think this remark deserved a comment, so she merely scowled at him in exasperation. He laughed again, then said, 'Okay, Merle, I'll stop teasing you. I used to babysit for pocket money when I was a teenager.' Lisa had snuggled against his shoulder, her eyes closing as she fell into an exhausted sleep.

'But why?'

'Why? I guess because I like kids.' Leon shrugged, taking the baby over to the car bed and laying her gently on her stomach. 'It was that or get a paper route,' he said, turning back to her.

'But why would you need money?' Merle asked, confused.

He gave her a mocking look. 'Merle, why does any teenage boy need money? So he can spend it on teenage girls,' he answered the question for her.

'But your father's wealthy.'

'He is?' His brows lifted, his eyes flashing with amusement. 'I'll have to tell him so he can quit his job with the government.'

'Your father's a civil servant?' Merle frowned. 'But everybody says . . .'

Leon's laughter interrupted her. 'You've been listening to gossip, Merle,' he accused her, still chuckling. 'That rumour got started when someone discovered I had the same last name as Sir Robert Crane who is very big in shipping or something. Because I had enough leverage to start up Puma Resources, they assumed I must of have got the money from him. It didn't help that my father is also named Robert, but if I am related to *Sir* Robert, I assure you it must be a very distant relationship. I've never even met the man.'

The boys came up as Merle was mulling over this bit of information and asked Leon if they could watch television again. They had picked up their toys, so he gave his permission, providing they could agree on which show to watch and kept the volume at a reasonable level. Sean looked like he would like to renew their argument over the choice of show, but his brother took one look at Leon's face and stifled him. Eventually, they compromised on an old rerun of a situation comedy and were soon happily engrossed in the antics of the Skipper and Gilligan.

Leon looked back at Merle and started to grin. 'Okay, out with it. I can see you're dying to ask me something.'

'Where *did* you get the money to start Puma?' Her forehead was pleated in a puzzled frown. Starting up an oil company wasn't exactly in the same league as opening a corner grocery store. It took a tremendous amount of capital to assemble the equipment and men needed for such an enterprise.

'The number fourteen,' Leon said simply.

'Fourteen?' Merle echoed, more confused than ever.

'Come on, I can see I'll have to tell you the story of my life.' He settled himself in one of the chairs and indicated that she should join him. Once Merle had sat down, he started to speak. 'I had been working in Saudi Arabia for about three years, and when I had some time off, I went to Monte Carlo to think over whether or not I wanted to stay in the Middle East. I was happy enough in the job, but I had been wanting to go out on my own for several years. I'd saved quite a bit of my salary over the years but even though I had a tidy sum of money, it wasn't anywhere near enough to start an oil exploration company, and I was starting to realise I would never save enough. One night in the casino, I decided what to do. I walked over to the roulette table and put my savings on number fourteen. If I won, I would have enough money to start my company. If I lost, I figured I would just go back to Saudi Arabia.'

'And you won?'

Leon nodded, grinning. 'It paid off at thirty-five to one. I took the money and came to Canada. The rest is, as they say, history.'

'But what if you had lost? It would have been all your savings.' Merle stared at him increduously.

'My savings weren't doing me any good.' He shrugged. 'Working for a salary, I could never hope to save up enough to start my own company if I spent the rest of my life trying. So I thought, what the hell?'

Merle frowned. 'I still don't see how you could have done it.'

'It was easy. I just walked over to the table and put the money down.' He flashed her a grin.

She ignored his taunt. 'Why fourteen?'

'There was this old lady sitting at the table. She had an enormous stack of chips in front of her. When she reached out to place her bets, I was amazed she could even lift her hand. She must have had ten rings on it, all set with huge stones. I've always had this theory that money breeds money, even when it's just luck that's involved. So, when she put some chips on number fourteen, that's where I put my money.'

'And you won,' Merle breathed, still finding it difficult to believe. 'Do you still gamble?'

'That's what the oil business is all about,' he said drily, enjoying the traces of thought that were flickering across Merle's face like neon lights. Taking pity on her, he continued, 'If you mean, do I still play roulette, the answer is no. I haven't been in a casino since. I don't even buy lottery tickets.'

Merle stared at him. What an incredible story! Maybe that was why he regarded the business of the well as nothing more than a game. 'This is a better story than the one about you coming from a wealthy family. I can't understand how come I haven't heard it before.'

'That's because you're the only person I have ever told,' Leon said matter-of-factly and Merle looked at him in surprise. His face was in profile as his eyes rested on the two boys sitting as though entranced in front of the television.

'You mean, nobody else knows?'

'That's right, and Merle, keep it quiet, will you? If it got around that that was where I got my money, I think my bank manager would start getting awfully nervous.' He turned his head and smiled at her, causing her heart to give a little jerk. It was gone, that barrier he had erected against her was missing. With all that had been going on when he had arrived she hadn't realised it before.

Merle wet her lips. She wanted to ask him if he had forgiven her but didn't have the courage. He must have done, though, for why else would he have told her his secret? Of course, the story might not even be true. It was a little far-fetched, even if it did sound like the sort of thing Leon might do.

He had gone back to watching the boys and Merle continued to stare at him. It was also the sort of story Leon might make up just to confound her, one of his practical jokes. Maybe he really was the son of Sir Robert, the shipping magnate.

'Leon,' she asked quietly, 'is this story true? I mean, did you really win the money to start Puma Resources?'

'Now why would I want to lie about a thing like that?' he asked, not quite answering the question and not taking his eyes from the boys.

'Because,' Merle said, frowning at him as her suspicions grew, 'you like teasing me.'

He grinned over at her. 'That's because you're so gullible.'

'Then it was all a lie?' she demanded, feeling a stab of disappointment.

'I didn't say that. I might have got the money that way, on the other hand, I might not. I could have rescued a sheikh's daughter from a fate worse than death and he gave me the money as a reward. After all, you know how I am when it comes to ladies in distress.' He glanced back at the boys. 'Speaking of which, have you given any thought to how you're going to feed those two?' he asked, deftly changing the subject.

'Andrew and Sean?' Merle followed his gaze. 'Not really. I guess I'll probably take them over to the truckstop in a little while.'

'Do you really think you can manage two small boys and a baby in a public restaurant?' he asked, his eyebrows lifting.

'Oh.' She hadn't thought about that. Merle glanced over at the car bed where Lisa was sleeping peacefully. What if she started screaming like she had earlier while they were at the café?

'Don't worry, Merle,' Leon cut into her thoughts, 'since it looks like you're in need of rescuing again, I'll help you. That seems to be my role in life. We'll move this lot over to my kitchen unit and we can fix them something to eat there.' He stood up and went over to enlist the boys' aid in making the move. 'Besides,' he said over his shoulder to Merle, 'you have to stick around the motel. I talked to the RCMP this afternoon and they're coming over to see you later.'

'They found out something?' Merle asked, surprised. She hadn't heard from the police since they had talked to her on the hill the morning after the shooting.

'No, but they want to ask you some more questions.' He turned off the television and told the boys to get their toys so they could move to the other unit.

'About what?'

'Greg Larson.'

'Greg? Why . . .?'

'Merle,' Leon said seriously, his eyes meeting hers and his expression grave as he turned to look at her, 'I suggested they might want to check him out. He *was* pretty angry with you the last time you saw him. He hit you.'

'He was in a temper. I think you're being ridiculous, Leon,' Merle dismissed his doubts. 'You, yourself, said there is a big difference between an act of passion and something done in cold blood. Greg Larson couldn't have had anything to do with those shots. It was a hunter.'

'You don't know that, Merle. I can't see any harm in letting the police check him out.'

'And while they do?' she asked suspiciously. She remembered the promise he had extracted from her and her nerves tightened. Was this another trick to stop her from scouting the well? When he didn't answer the question she had just put to him, she asked, 'Have you made a decision on the well?'

'We have.'

'And?'

Leon sighed. 'The drilling resumes tomorrow.'

'And I suppose I'm to stay away from the site while

the police check out this latest theory of yours, is that it?'

'I know what you're trying to get at, Merle, but believe me I'm not using this as an excuse to stop you from scouting the well. I honestly believe that Larson should be checked out.'

'I think I understand, Leon,' Merle said coldly. 'Okay, I'll talk to the police, but I don't consider that promise I gave to you still binding. If *they* are as concerned about Greg as you pretend to be, I won't go out. But, if they're not, then I think this is just another one of your dirty tricks.'

His only answer was the tightening of his jaw as his eyes grew cold. He turned away abruptly and started helping the boys gather their belongings, his movements made stiff with caged anger.

Although he continued to assist her in the care of the children throughout the evening, Leon made sure the newly resurrected wall between them remained firmly intact. He allowed Merle to take over the kitchen unit temporarily and moved his things into Mrs Blake's room.

Later, the manageress dropped by to inform them that Mrs Blake had had an emergency appendectomy and that he husband was driving out from Calgary to join her. Fortunately, the couple had friends who would be arriving at the motel in the morning to take the children into their care while their mother was incapacitated.

Leon's latent anger erupted after they had given little Lisa her bath. Being totally unfamiliar with the procedure, Merle had none the less gamely set out to clean her charge. Unfortunately, Lisa did not want to be cleaned and proceeded to give her opinion of a bath at the top of her lungs. As seemed to happen all too frequently, Leon came to Merle's rescue, taking over the squalling infant and finishing the task with a deftness that left Merle astounded.

When the baby had been settled for a sleep, Merle decided to tell Leon she would do as he asked and stay away from the hilltop. The police had arrived shortly after they had eaten and questioned her about her relationship with Greg Larson. It had been an embarrassing interview. Apparently, they had already talked to the men working on the rig and she was placed in the position of having to refute Greg's story as to the nature of their friendship. She could sense their scepticism as they heard her out, but also sensed that they were just as sceptical of Leon's theory that Greg was the one who had shot at her. Nonetheless, they promised to investigate.

Their lack of suspicion regarding Greg Larson temporarily strengthened her resolve to go back to the hilltop, but after she had thought it over she decided she was just being stubborn. She had more or less decided she wasn't going to turn her report on the well over to Wild Rose, so continuing to scout it was rather pointless. In the back of her mind, Merle also cherished the hope that by giving in to Leon on this she might be able to mend the rift between them. If it didn't, then perhaps the best thing for everyone concerned would be for her to go back to Calgary and try to get on with the rest of her life.

Merle left Lisa sleeping soundly in her car bed in the bedroom and went back into the living room. The boys had gone to bed earlier, their protests that they weren't the least bit tired negated by the speed with which they fell asleep. Leon was standing by the sink, wiping away the water that had splashed out while they were bathing the baby.

'Leon, I have something to tell you,' Merle opened the conversation.

He turned around, a fed-up look in his eyes. 'Do you? Well, guess what? I don't want to hear it. I'm sick to the teeth with you, lady. You'd rather get yourself killed than leave that well alone. Well, I have something to tell you. You are not going out to that hill again. I forbid it.'

'Forbid it?' Merle asked, astonishment at the suddenness of his attack quickly turning to outrage. Nobody *forbade* her to do anything!

'That's right. I've taken the liberty of lifting your car keys again, so don't get any ideas about driving out there tomorrow. I suppose you could walk, but I think you'll be sorry if you do.' He tossed the cloth he had been using on to the counter and stalked to the door, then turned back to her. 'I doubt if Lisa will sleep through the night, so you had better get some sleep while you can.' With that final piece of advice, he stalked out of the unit, slamming the door behind him.

'Damn Leon, damn him, damn him, *damn* him,' Merle muttered as she tramped up the hillside, viciously kicking out at any obstructions that lay in her path. She had absolutely no desire to be up on this *damn* hill, but he had backed her into a corner. Even after last night, she still might have been able to retreat and retain a modicum of pride, but not now.

This morning, Leon had arrived at the kitchen unit as Merle was preparing breakfast for Sean and Andrew. No sooner had he walked in than Lisa had started crying so he had taken over the preparation of the meal while Merle attended to the baby. (Which was *another* thing she didn't like about him. Every time he showed up, something went wrong and he would end up taking charge as though she were totally incapable of handling the problem herself. She was sick to death of being treated like the village idiot!)

His manner throughout breakfast had been arrogant and faintly taunting, almost daring her to mention the well. Although his attitude infuriated her no end, Merle managed to hold her tongue. It wasn't as though they could conduct a slanging match in front of the children. Then, the couple who were taking charge of the children had arrived and everything else was forgotten in a flurry of preparations for their departure.

To Merle's relief, the couple, John and Candice Burton, were not strangers to the boys. Until six months ago, the Burtons had lived in the same city in Ontario as the Blakes. Both Andrew and Sean remembered them and seemed content to be placed in their care.

While Merle had grown attached to the boys while they were in her charge, it was Lisa's departure that brought a hard lump to her throat. It was so bewildering. She had been up with the baby every three hours throughout the night, changing her and feeding her, making sure she burped her before returning her to the car bed. Merle just couldn't understand why she would miss her but she knew she would.

After the car bearing the children drove away, Merle felt flat and dispirited—and certainly not in the mood for a phone call from her mother. Leon had got in touch with her again. Merle found nothing funny in this latest interference in her life. Though her mother loved nothing better than to advise Merle on how she should conduct her life, fortunately she was blessed with a short memory and generally forgot about her daughter—unless something or *somebody* reminded her.

Admittedly, her mother had been concerned that Merle might be in danger, but that hadn't stopped her from jumping to some pretty wild conclusions about Merle's relationship with Leon. Nor had she refrained from delivering a lecture on the unattractiveness of women who were too independent. Men didn't like women who were constantly defying them, and Merle had better revise her attitude or Leon was going to slip through her fingers.

Merle was furious by the time she finally got off the phone. Dragging Edith into their disagreement had been totally unwarranted—and if Leon thought that having her mother on his side was going to change anything, he could think again. Picking the lock on the Blazer wasn't as easy as she had hoped, but after about fifteen minutes she managed it. Once she was in the cab, she found the wires that ran to the ignition and within seconds the motor was running. Maybe she could become a car thief when she gave up scouting, she thought sardonically as she drove off. Of course, she would have to improve her lock-picking skills. She had got some very suspicious looks from departing guests while she was trying to open the door to the Blazer.

When Merle had climbed to the crest of the hill, she stood peering down at the site. The drilling had resumed as expected and even at this distance she could detect the faint odour of natural gas that hung in the air. The gas was escaping as the bit passed through the bearing layers.

She saw Leon standing near the rig and remained where she was until he noticed her. When he finally glanced up at the hilltop, Merle waved a salute, then settled down to take up her position. While standing, she hadn't bothered with the binoculars: she could imagine quite clearly what Leon's expression would be on seeing her, and smiled to herself. God, she loved it when she outsmarted him and so far this summer that hadn't happened very often.

She had been lying on the hilltop for nearly an hour when she heard a noise behind her. Every nerve in her body went on red alert. She didn't really believe in Leon's assertion that Greg Larson might be trying to harm her, but subconsciously it had been preying on her mind. Telling herself it was ridiculous to be nervous, she slowly lowered the binoculars she had been holding and turned to peer over her shoulder.

It was a dog—*that* dog. This is what Leon had meant when he said she would be sorry if she came out. For several seconds, Merle stared into the small, beady eyes watching her. Her hand was trembling as she reached it out to him. 'Nice, d-dog . . . nice Laddie Boy,' she whispered. Laddie Boy curled his lip and a growl rumbled in his throat. Merle snatched her hand back, her heart thundering in her chest.

The dog took a step towards her and her chest tightened in panic. Her instinct was to flee, to jump up and run away as fast as she could, but she knew that would be fatal. The dog would be on her in seconds. Calm down, Merle, she ordered herself. Think!

She knew that if you came on a bear when working in the bush, you were supposed to play dead. She didn't know if it worked for dogs, but she lowered her head to the ground and covered it with her arms. Her pulse was pounding like a jack-hammer as the seconds ticked by. All she could think about were sharp fangs burying themselves into her flesh.

She felt something nuzzle her leg and knew the dog

had come over to her. Laddie Boy ran his nose up her thigh, occasionally prodding her with one of his huge paws. When he reached her midriff, Merle felt a shiver run through her and goose bumps sprang out on her arms. Lord, what a time to get ticklish!

A cold, wet nose was shoved into her ear and Merle closed her eyes tight, sure the dog would be sinking his teeth into her at any moment. They flew open again when Laddie Boy started washing her neck with his tongue. Cautiously, she turned her head slightly to eye him warily. The tongue hit her full in the face, sliding wetly over her mouth. 'Stop that, you stupid dog,' she ordered automatically.

Laddie Boy cocked his head and he stared down at her. He growled softly, then started washing her face again. Merle sat up and the big dog climbed into her lap, still intent on licking her face. She shoved him away and he flopped down beside her, thumping his tail against the ground as he looked up at her.

'You got me all wet, you idiot,' Merle said, digging into her pocket for a handkerchief. At the sound of her voice, Laddie Boy bared his teeth, his tail beating faster. Merle stared at the dog, frowning. 'Is that how you smile?. The dog growled, then stood up, his tongue going for her face.

Merle laughed, pushing him away. 'Stop that! Okay, I believe you, you're a friendly dog.' She twisted her head to evade that sopping tongue. She finally managed to get the dog to lie down again and sat with him, idly scratching him behind the ears. Leon must know the dog was friendly. No wonder he had practically died laughing when she had seen him in the truckstop after first meeting Laddie Boy and she had been so obviously frightened of the animal. So why had he sent it up here? Of course, maybe he hadn't, but somehow this had all the earmarks of a Leon Crane prank.

Merle stared down at the dog. Maybe Leon had thought she wouldn't stay around long enough to find out the dog was friendly. That was probably it. He didn't want her up here so he had sent the dog to scare her off. 'Well, Laddie Boy, I think I might just have scored another point.' She laughed, hugging the animal. 'Two in one day, that has to be a record.'

CHAPTER TEN

LADDIE BOY lay in the October sunshine letting its warmth soak through his heavy coat of black fur. His head rested on his paws and one ear twitched as a fly, made sluggish by the cool autumn weather, buzzed past. The fly continued to annoy him and he opened his eyes, his muscles tensing when he saw the jackrabbit. The hare had not seen him yet, and he waited for it to move closer before springing into action. Laddie Boy trembled in anticipation, watching as the jackrabbit's powerful haunches brought it a foot closer. Suddenly the hare sat upright, its nose twitching. It had caught his scent, and the dog leapt to his feet. The jackrabbit took off like a shot with Laddie Boy hard on his heels.

'Don't be too long,' Merle called to him over her shoulder. 'They're just about to run the drill stem test.' She turned her head back towards the drilling site but didn't lift the spotting scope back to her eye. Talking to the dog was a silly habit, and yet, one she didn't want to break. During the long days on the hilltop she had spent hours in conversation with Laddie Boy, talking about the well, Leon, life in general—not that he had much to say in response.

How had she missed dogs up until now? Laddie Boy was the first dog she had ever really noticed. Before him, the only dogs she had ever had contact with were guard dogs at some of the sites she scouted (which she regarded as just one more difficulty to overcome) or leashed animals being walked by their owners on city streets. She had never seen them as companions, friends.

Merle looked down at the spotting scope. Lately, she had been wondering if her whole life hadn't been viewed through the scope, with an oil well always in the lens. She just hadn't seen anything else, like dogs . . . like children . . . her mind drifting back to Lisa. She had cared for the infant for less than twenty-four hours, yet she had found a permanent niche in Merle's heart. Mary Blake had sent a note after she had recovered from her operation, including a snapshot of the children. Merle had taken the photo into Medicine Hat and had had it enlarged and framed. Now it rested on her dresser back at the motel.

Merle touched her stomach, wondering how it feel to be carrying Leon's child. That morning she hadn't guarded against pregnancy, hadn't even thought of it for that matter. When there had been no repercussions, she had been relieved but she wasn't so sure now. Not that she would use pregnancy to force him into marriage, but his baby would be something of him to hold to in the years to come.

Sighing, Merle returned the scope to her eye, centring the cross hairs on Leon. He had been out to check on the well intermittently since ordering her off the hill, and this week he had been there constantly, because of the numerous tests they had been conducting. Because they both stayed at the motel and frequented the truckstop, it had been inevitable that they see one another. When they passed in the hall or happened to sit at adjacent tables at the café, Leon looked right through her. She could have been invisible for all the notice he took of her.

She wasn't quite sure what she had been expecting when she had defied him over going out to the hill, but she hadn't expected him to ignore her. Over the past few weeks she had been developing a greater understanding of herself, and she strongly suspected that she had wanted him to somehow force her to obey him. That he hadn't showed her just how clearly she had destroyed any feelings he might have had for her.

At least there hadn't been any trouble in the past weeks. Though she hadn't spoken with the police again, she no longer had any fears for her safety. The days on the hilltop were peaceful and the drilling crew had even stopped annoying her when she went into the truckstop for her meals. Although it seemed out of character, she sometimes wondered if part of Leon's attitude towards her wasn't merely a stubborn refusal to admit he was wrong. He wouldn't admit his mistake even to the extent of returning her car keys. Finally after hot wiring the Blazer for two weeks, Merle had driven it into the GMC dealership in Medicine Hat and got another set of keys.

Leon was talking to the geologist and Merle moved the glass to look at the cellar, the ten-foot square concrete-lined hole at the base of the derrick. About six feet deep, its function was to accommodate some of the wellhead equipment and reduce the height of the rig. The roughnecks were there securing the last section of pipe, and Leon signalled the order to open the valve that would permit the oil, thousands of feet below the ground, to flow into the pipe. This was the third drill stem test in the past six days and Merle knew they were finding something. She could tell a lot about how things were going just by watching the faces of the men as they read the results.

As soon as the well was finished she would go back to Calgary and find a job. Since she wouldn't be handing in a report to Wild Rose and couldn't even pay them back the salary they had been paying her over the summer, she knew she wouldn't be able to find another scouting job. She really didn't care. Since meeting the Blake children she had decided she would like to do something that involved children. Not that she thought anyone would be fool enough to hire her to look after their offspring, but she could try to get a job as a school secretary, or something similar.

Although she was no longer scouting the well, she still watched it from the hill each day. Once it was in she wouldn't be able to see Leon again, even at a distance. He would go back to his offices in Calgary, and oil wasn't going to be a part of her future. She needed these last images of him to carry her through the rest of her life.

Merle heard a deep rumble coming from within the bowels of the earth and kept the spotting scope focused on the end of the drilling pipe. The thunderous sound grew louder and . . .

'Holy Sweet . . .' Merle's exclamation died in her throat as she almost dropped the scope. Never in the six years she had been scouting had she witnessed anything like this. 'My God!' She pressed the end of the scope more firmly against her eye. Oil was spewing out the end of the pipe in a fountain seventy feet high. It was a gusher, an old-fashioned gusher. Good Lord, she thought, this only happens in the movies.

The men at the site were going crazy, running and jumping around, letting the oil shower over them. Merle moved the scope, trying to find Leon among the medley. The men were becoming covered in crude and she couldn't spot him among the gyrating, black bodies. Puma No 14—*fourteen*! Had he expected something like this?

Merle turned her attention back to the plume of oil,

staring at it in fascination. 'Incredible,' she breathed, unable to take her eyes away from the black jet.

She didn't know how long she had been lying there staring at the gusher when she heard a noise behind her. 'Laddie Boy, come over here. You have to have a look at this,' she called to the dog, her eyes still riveted on the derrick. 'Come on, Laddie Boy, what's keeping you? This is a lot more exciting than some dumb rabbit.'

What was the matter with that dog? Usually he couldn't wait to come slobbering all over her. Finally, Merle turned around to see what he was doing and looked straight into Greg Larson's cold blue eyes.

Crude, high grade black crude.

Three hundred and fifty million years ago, a great shallow sea had covered this area of southern Alberta. Its slow-moving waters teamed with life, its shores were edged by huge primeval forests. The sea bed was covered in thick, black mud: *sapropel* from the Greek for rotten sea. The mud contained the decomposing remains of millions of marine plants and animals. As the eons passed and the sea retreated, the organic remains of these ancient life forms slowly broke down into long chains of carbon and hydrogen atoms. Impermeable shale overlaid the claystone that formed from the sea mud, trapping the hydrocarbons. At some point, these beds folded and the molecules migrated together to form one huge reservoir of crude.

Leon, unlike his men, didn't rush to the derrick to shower in the spray that had its origins so long ago. Nonetheless, his grin nearly split his oil-spattered face. *This* was what he had been hoping for. All the signs had been there, including the vague premonition that number fourteen would do it again. He had almost given up weeks ago when Merle had defied him about staying off the hill, but even for her, he hadn't been able to abandon the well.

He turned to look up towards the hill. In the past weeks she hadn't even tried to conceal her surveillance activities and he had spent many hours watching her from the office window. His grin faded when he didn't see her. Perhaps she had left, defeated because she would know now that all her reports would be worthless. A find of this sort was not something that could be concealed. By this evening, all of Alberta would have heard of the gusher, by tomorrow, the rest of the world.

He turned to look back at the fountain of oil. In a few minutes, he would give the order to have the men cap the well, but for now, he just wanted to stare at it, to let the feeling of accomplishment swell inside him. It was a once-in-a-lifetime event. In the years to come, there would be plenty of dry holes and mediocre finds to cope with. He wanted to savour this moment of triumph a little while longer.

The security guard from the gate came over and tapped him on the shoulder. 'Some cops are here and they want to talk to you.'

'The police?' Leon questioned, the well momentarily forgotten. 'Did they say what they wanted?'

The guard dragged his eyes away from the black column of petroleum. 'Nope, just said they wanted to see you. Shall I tell them to come back later?'

'No, I'll talk to them now.' Leon started towards the gate, glancing up at the hill as he walked. He felt uneasy. Where the hell was Merle? It wasn't like her to slink off with her tail between her legs just because her job had proved fruitless.

He recognised the two officers as the ones who had

spoken to Merle that morning after the shooting, and his foreboding increased. They were staring transfixed at the crude shooting over the top of the derrick.

The corporal turned to him when he reached the gate. 'That's really something,' he said, gesturing to the rig. 'Guess you must be used to it, but I've never seen anything like it.' He turned his attention back to the derrick.

'You wanted to talk to me?' Leon asked impatiently.

Reluctantly, the police officer looked back at him. 'Yeah, we're looking for Merle Halliday. We thought you might know where we could find her?'

'You found out something?' Leon queried sharply.

'Well, it looks like your hunch about Larson might have been right. We can't place him at the shooting, but we've found out some interesting things about him and thought maybe we should have another talk with Miss Halliday.'

His eyes kept flicking back to the well and Leon felt his irritation increase. 'What kind of interesting things?'

'It seems Larson spent a few months in a mental hospital some years back. The doctor we talked to said they would have liked to have kept him longer but as he had committed himself voluntarily, they couldn't stop him from leaving.'

'This doctor thinks he could be dangerous?'

'It's a possibility.' He paused, still distracted by the well. 'That's why we want to find Miss Halliday. We can't find Larson,' the officer added, matter-of-factly.

'What do you mean, you can't find Larson?' Leon demanded.

'Just that, he's disappeared. Apparently, he arranged for another job after you fired him, but never showed up for work.' The officer looked at Leon curiously. If that was *his* well pouring oil out like that, he wouldn't be wasting his time worrying about some dame. He looked back at the gush of oil. He had no idea what it was worth but if his heating bills last winter were anything to go by, he bet Crane could buy just about any woman he wanted after a strike like this.

'Merle's usually up on that hill.' Leon pointed to the hilltop, forcing the officer's attention back to him. 'I haven't seen her for a few minutes, but I've had a man keeping an eye on her since the shooting. We can get him on the mobile phone and see where she went.' The security guard was standing a few feet away, watching his fellow employees cavorting in the black shower, and Leon called over to him, 'Joe, get Ed Daily on the phone for me.'

'Don't have to do that, Mr Crane.' The guard gestured to the men over by the rig. 'He came tearing in here a few minutes after the well blew. Guess he didn't want to miss all the excitement.'

'He did *what?*'

Joe's eyes flew to his boss's face. He looked like he was about to murder someone. By and large, Mr Crane was an easy-going employer, but Joe knew he could only be pushed so far. When that geologist, Larson, had ignored his orders, Crane had fired him without a qualm. From the looks of the boss now, old Ed was going to have to start looking for another job as well. 'Do you want me to go get him?' The guard shifted uneasily on his feet. He hoped the boss wasn't going to get mad at *him.*

'I'll deal with him later,' Leon snapped, turning to the policemen. 'Let's get up to that hill and see what the hell's happened to her.'

Merle's eyes kept going to the rifle, drawn to it like a

migrating salmon going to its spawning grounds. *How long before he used it?* She forced herself to look back at Greg's face, to make sense of his rambling. He had been talking for hours, it seemed. His monologue was disjointed, the ravings of a mad man. One point was clear, though: he intended to use that rifle.

She tried to focus on his words, to make some sense of this nightmare, to find some lifeline out of it. He was talking about his childhood and tears started pouring down his cheeks. Impatiently, he brushed them away with his sleeve. As he spoke, Merle realised he was starting to confuse her with his mother, laying the blame for childhood slights and disappointments at her door.

They were sitting on the ground, facing one another, a few feet from the crest of the hill and out of sight of the well. She realised that Leon must have had someone keeping an eye on her, because Greg had said that he had been watching her for weeks, waiting for the man to leave her alone so he could approach her. Laddie Boy had never returned from chasing the hare and she wondered if Greg had done something to the dog. In spite of her own fears, she couldn't help feeling concern for the animal.

At first, Merle had made some attempt to reason with him, to talk him out of this course he was so determinedly set upon. Merle shuddered slightly when she thought of the gusher. She had sought to distract him by drawing his attention to it. That's when she realised just how truly unbalanced he was was. He had become incensed at the mention of the well and for a moment, Merle thought he would shoot her right then. He seemed to think the well should have belonged to him, that it was Leon's only because Merle had lost him his job.

Now, Merle sat in frozen silence as he talked and talked. Occasionally, he fingered the safety catch on the rifle, the faint clicking sound as he snapped it on and off sending icy shafts of terror through Merle's heart. In his distorted mind everything that had ever gone wrong in his life was focused on her—and the only way he could exorcise the devils that plagued him was to kill her.

The occasional sob was disrupting his speech now, and Merle suddenly realised he wasn't watching her as intently as he had been. Gradually, his words were growing muffled and he lowered his head, wiping away the tears from his face with one hand.

Merle felt her muscles tighten. Should she try to make a run for it? Greg was muttering to himself and hadn't looked back up at her. Merle shifted slightly, tensed for his reaction. When he didn't look up, she slowly rearranged her legs so she could spring to her feet. Her eyes went back to the rifle. If she ran, she couldn't afford to think about it. She would just have to run and keep on running, and not think about the bullets that might stop her.

She closed her eyes, taking a deep breath. When she opened her eyes again, he was still talking to himself, his head bowed. Now!

In one motion, Merle was on her feet and running in a broken pattern down the hill, dodging clumps of sage and rocks. She heard Greg shout, the crack of the rifle being fired, but didn't ease her pace. This was her only chance and she couldn't afford to think about anything stopping her. Her lungs were burning, her heart thundering in her chest. Her ankle twisted as she landed after jumping over a bush, but she ignored the pain. She had to keep running, reach the Blazer and get away.

She was so intent on escape that at first she didn't recognise the men coming up the hill towards her as anything but more obstacles in her path. Then she saw Leon break into a run towards her. She swerved, heading straight for him and launched herself into the arms he held out to her.

Her breath came in ragged sobs as she felt the warm, hard security of those arms fold around her. Merle buried her face in his hard chest, uncaring that his shirt reaked of crude oil and that his pulse was racing as quickly as her own. She was safe. Her heart was gradually slowing to normal, her breathing becoming easier. 'Oh, Leon, you were r-right,' she stammered. 'He wanted to k-kill me.'

'It's okay now, he can't hurt you.' Leon murmured gently, holding her tighter. 'The police will take care of him.'

'He has a gun, he's crazy.' Merle shuddered against his chest, burying her face deeper into the folds of his shirt. She heard Leon talking to the police officers. They had heard the shot and one of them went to call for reinforcements. Then Leon led her to his Blazer and after opening the door, helped her on to the bench seat. Joining her, he pulled her back to his chest, understanding her need for comforting arms.

When she was calmer, Merle said softly, 'I should have listened to you. You were right. I just didn't want to give in to you. I'll never defy you again,' she promised, her voice filled with deep emotion.

Leon laughed softly, amused by her uncharacteristic docility. Holding her slightly away from him, he looked down into her face. Now that the ordeal was over, her eyes were misted with tears that threatened to spill down her cheeks. One side of her face was streaked with black oil from his shirt, stark against her still pale countenance. He had never seen anyone so beautiful. 'That, my love, is a promise I am *not* going to let you renege on.'

He dropped his head, his mouth seeking hers. She clung to him, letting the tenderness and comfort of his kiss purge the terror of the last hour. His lips explored her with all the pent-up longing of the weeks since she had lain in his arms. His hands pulled her pliant form closer to his hard one as though he would take her into his heart where she would forever be safe. When he released her, she lay weakly against his chest.

For several minutes they sat in silence. More police cars pulled up to join the one that was parked behind the Blazer. Merle shuddered anew as she saw the officers climbing the hill carrying rifles. Despite the nightmare, she could still feel deep pity for Greg Larson and did not want to see him hurt.

In the end, Greg Larson's capture proved to be an anticlimax. The police found him standing at the crest of the hill, crying and muttering to himself as he stared down at the well site. His gun was lying on the ground a few feet away and though he attempted to reach it when he realised the police were there, they had little difficulty in restraining him. His resistence crumbled completely once he was hand-cuffed and he docilely let the officers lead him down the hill, tears streaming down his face. The police allowed Leon to drive Merle to the station, following behind the squad car bearing Greg Larson. Though she had to give a statement, it appeared unlikely that Larson would ever be fit to stand trial.

Several hours later, Leon parked the Blazer at the side of the gravel road that ran along the base of the hill. They had returned to the motel and changed, then had dinner together at the truckstop. Neither of them had mentioned the well or Greg Larson. Instead, they spoke of inconsequentials, their conversation potholed with long silences. Now that it was all over, the familiar coolness had crept between them again.

'Leon,' Merle said softly, 'I don't want to go back up there.'

'You have to, Merle,' he said firmly. 'You have to face what happened up there and come to terms with it.'

'But Leon . . .'

'No buts, Merle,' he said sternly, opening the door to the cab. 'You promised not to defy me—I'm holding you to it. Don't worry, I'll be with you.'

He got out and came around the front of the Blazer to help her out. The sun had set hours ago, but the landscape was bright from the light of the harvest moon. The air was chill and already hoar frost was painting the prairie white. Leon joined her, and with his arm about her shoulders, they silently climbed the hill. In the distance, a coyote yelped and a dog started to bark. Merle bit her lip, wondering what had happened to Laddie Boy.

Merle's heat was pounding heavily in her chest when they reached the crest of the hill, and not from the exertion of the climb. But Leon was right, she had to face it. If she didn't she might never feel safe again.

Leon moved a few feet away to peer down at the well site, while Merle stood staring at the spot where Greg Larson had been. She felt a deep compassion for the man—and guilt. What role had she played in his breakdown? Though the police had assured her that he had been unstable long before she came into her life, she knew that she was not totally blameless in precipitating the events of this afternoon. For several minutes she thought about Greg, about the way she had led him on. She thought of all the other men she had known over the years. She had always told herself she needn't feel guilty for using them. They hadn't been hurt. In exchange for some pleasant companionship, they gave her information. But, now, she knew she had been lying to herself. Of course they had suffered emotional pain when they discovered what she was about! She just hadn't wanted to admit it.

She looked over to Leon. He had found her spotting scope, which she had left on the hill, and was using it to look at the drilling site. She would have used him, too, if he had let her. That was probably why she had been so angry with him most of the summer. And, that was why they would be saying goodbye tonight.

Leon lowered the scope and turned to her, holding out his hand to her. With slow steps, Merle went to him but didn't accept his hand.

Standing apart, they stared down at the drilling site. The men had capped the well now, but pools of black crude still surrounded the derrick. The site was illuminated by powerful overhead lamps, their reflected light breaking into prisms on the surface of the puddles.

'I saw the strike,' Merle said quietly. 'It was ... incredible. I'd never seen anything like it before.'

'To tell you the truth, neither had I,' Leon admitted. 'You know what it means, though, don't you? Your report won't do Wild Rose much good now. Every company in the country will be bidding on those available leases after this.'

'It doesn't matter,' she muttered, keeping her eyes turned to the well.

'Doesn't it?' he asked, hardness creeping into his voice. 'You risked your life for that report.'

Merle shook her head slightly. 'I—I'd changed my

mind about turning in my report.' She shrugged, trying, and failing, to smile at him.

'When did you decide that?' he asked and Merle sensed a strange tension in him as he waited for her answer.

'A while ago,' she answered, lightly. She knew he had turned his head to look at her and for a second she held his eyes, before hastily lowering them, but then looked back. What did it matter if he guessed she loved him? It was all over between them now. Knowing the sort of person she was, she could see now he would never return her love.

'Why were you still watching the well?'

Merle ignored the question, looking back to the site. 'I ... Larson, oh, Leon I feel so badly about what happened. It was my fault.'

'We all make mistakes, Merle.'

'You don't understand, Leon,' Merle protested, driven on by shame and guilt. 'Greg wasn't the first man that I used. Practically every job, I found someone I could pump. I told myself that I wasn't hurting them. I thought because I wasn't sleeping with them, I was keeping everything nice and light. But some of those guys were in love with me and I just walked away from them as soon as the well was finished. Most of the time, I couldn't even remember their names after I left.'

Leon set the scope down and put his hands on her shoulders, turning her to face him. 'Merle, we've all done things we've regretted, that we're ashamed of. It's not easy to learn to live with guilt and remorse, but you have no choice. The only thing you can do, is try to change.'

'Oh, Leon, it's ... it's different for you.'

'Don't you think I have faults?' He mocked her

gently, pulling her to him. 'Merle, I've done things I've regretted afterwards. Anyone who is human has. How do you think I felt after forcing you to take that money? I threatened to break your arm ... I still haven't forgiven myself for that. I've always despised men who use their superior strength against women, and yet ... I did the very thing I hate.' Merle rested against his hard chest, his heart beating steadily in her ear.

'Merle,' he said softly, 'we can't change the past, only try not to make the same mistakes in the future. You know when you asked me where I got the money to start Puma Resources and I told you the story about winning it?'

She nodded.

'It didn't happen quite like that, although I did win the money. I told you that story because I wasn't sure I was ready to tell you the whole truth—or that you were ready to hear it. Besides which, you're so gullible I enjoy teasing you.' He smoothed her hair in a tender gesture. 'To be honest, I went into that casino to lose the money, although it didn't end up that way.'

Merle leaned away from him and peered into his face. 'You'll have to explain.'

'While I was in the Middle East I was engaged to a girl in London. Every few months I would fly back to England and spend a few days with her, then return to my job. It wasn't a very satisfactory arrangement, but I could make far more working overseas than I could if I stayed in Britain. You see, I very badly wanted to have my own company, so I was saving every penny that I could. Well, to make a long story short, my fiancée got tired of waiting. She wanted to get married, and I wanted to wait until I had enough money to start my own company. We had a big row about it and the next time I went back to see her, she was married to someone else.' He fell silent for a few minutes and Merle snuggled closer to him. She wondered what the woman had been like. She sensed that it still hurt Leon to talk about her and envy snaked through her. The woman had been a fool to give him up.

'It was my obsession with starting my own compnay that cost me the girl I loved,' he said softly, then held her away from him so he could look into her face. 'So I do know how you're feeling now. I hurt the woman I loved—and lost her—because I let ambition override everything else.'

'But Leon, I've been so wicked.'

'No, Merle.' He shook his head, smiling gently down at her. 'Not wicked, just very unthinking. You didn't set out to maliciously hurt Greg—you just didn't consider the consequences of what you were doing. You've had a painful lesson, but one you needed to learn.'

Merle rested her head in the hollow below his shoulder, considering his words. She derived comfort from them. She knew she would be different in the future. Perhaps because she had never been hurt herself before loving Leon, she hadn't been able to comprehend the hurt she could inflict on others.

After a few minutes, she said, 'Leon, I still don't understand about the money.'

'When I discovered I had lost Louise, I guess I went a little crazy. I left London immediately and ended up in Monte Carlo. I suppose it was some sort of idea for self-punishment, but I suddenly felt I had to get rid of all the money I had saved. I wired my bank in London and had my savings transferred to Monte and took the whole works into the casino one night. Then . . .' Leon chuckled. 'You remember the lady with the rings?' Merle nodded. 'Well, she hadn't been winning, in fact, she was just about out of chips. Since I wanted to lose, I placed my bets where she did—only her luck changed just then, and we both started to win.'

'Why didn't you just keep playing until you started losing?' Merle asked, puzzled.

He looked down at her, his expression chastening. 'Merle, I'm impulsive, not stupid. When I saw how much money I had won, I came to my senses and stopped playing. My company has never been an adequate substitute for what I could have had with Louise, but it's been satisfying, nonetheless.'

He had wanted to marry a woman named Louise. Just the way Leon had said the name, Merle knew he had loved her. Paul—after they broke up, Merle had realised she hadn't even liked him very much, much less loved him. 'Do you still love her?' Merle asked softly, compelled by some masochistic need to know.

Leon sighed. 'Not the same way I did when I was engaged to her, but, in a way, yes. You never completely forget someone you were that close to. I think we could have been happy together.'

'I see,' Merle said slowly, the pain of jealousy almost suffocating her. 'Would you marry her now—if you could, that is?'

'No, I wouldn't,' he said simply. His mouth brushed hers and he continued, 'Because I'm going to buy a horse . . . and marry you.'

Merle pulled away from him. 'You're going to what?'

'I'm going to buy a horse. A white one, I think.' He grinned down at her confused countenance. 'I was so slow rescuing you this afternoon, you had to rescue yourself. I don't want that to happen after we're married, so I figure I had better get a horse.'

'You want to marry me?' Merle asked in amazement, joy starting to beat a heavy tattoo in her chest.

'You *are* in love with me, aren't you?' he mocked. 'Isn't that why you decided against turning in your report?'

'But . . . of course . . .'

'Of course,' he interrupted, claiming her lips briefly. 'And since I'm in love with you, then don't you think we should get married? You know your mother will drive us both crazy if we don't.'

'I . . . you were so angry with me after we made love.'

'That morning I knew how I felt about you, but I still wasn't sure of how you felt about me. I suppose that's why I just asked you to live with me instead of marrying me, which was what I really wanted. Then, God,' he swore softly, 'you brought up the well . . . Damn it Merle, I knew Larson thought you loved him. God knows how many men have *thought* you loved them over the years. I could see myself in this long queue of men who thought Merle Halliday loved them when all Merle Halliday loved was her job.'

Merle pressed closer to him, aware of the bitterness in his words. 'Oh, Leon, I'm sorry. When you got so angry, I knew I had been wrong to accuse you like that but I didn't know how to make things right. But, believe me, I did love you then. It was just that my job had been my whole life for so long that I saw everything in relationship to it.'

He twined his fingers through the silk of her hair, and when he spoke his voice was rough. 'When I found you had been shot at, I started to realise that it didn't really matter how you felt about me. I loved you and I couldn't stand the idea of you being hurt even if you had only been using me. I wanted to protect you—except you wouldn't let me. By the way, how *did* you get the Blazer running?'

'I hot wired it.'

'Where did you learn to do a thing like that?'

Merle shrugged. 'From a guy I used to date. He was kind of a shady character.'

Leon scowled at her. 'I think I'd better marry you pretty quick. The sooner you're out of circulation the better. You pick some real winners for boyfriends.' He saw the shadow that crossed her face, and cursing himself for the careless remark, pulled her to his chest. It would take a long time for Merle to come to terms with her role in Greg Larson's breakdown, to forgive herself for what she had done.

'Leon,' Merle asked quietly, a few minutes later, her lips softly swollen from the thorough kiss Leon had just administered. 'Do you think we could have children when we're married? I know you would have to teach me how to take care of them, but I . . . I miss Lisa and the boys.'

He chuckled softly. 'My dear, I fully intend to keep you barefoot and pregnant for the next few years. It will keep you from going out scouting oil wells.'

'You're a chauvinist, Leon,' Merle accused, but her eyes were smiling. If any other man had said that to her, she would have been furious. With Leon, she was actually looking forward to the prospect.

'You got it. Now, let's get back to the motel, so I can get started.' With their arms around each other's waists, they started back to the truck. Half-way down the hill, Leon stopped.

'Did you hear something?'

Merle had and started to grin. 'Laddie Boy!' she

called. The big dog came bounding up. He growled at Leon, then jumped up and with his big paws on Merle's shoulders, started washing her face. 'Stop that, you big lump,' she cried, pushing him down. He sat on his haunches, his tail thumping, his teeth bared while Merle knelt down and hugged him. 'You missed all the excitement, boy,' she scolded him and he replied with a deep growl. If he could only explain about that rabbit—he had *almost* caught it this time.

'It looks like I'm going to have to buy a bigger house,' Leon laughed down at her. Merle looked up at him questioningly. 'We're going to need a lot of room to keep that dog, the horse, and all the kids we're going to have,' he explained.

'Do you think the man who owns him would let us have him?'

'It wouldn't surprise me if he wouldn't pay us to take him off his hands,' he said, laughing as he reached down and lifted her to her feet. 'Come on, I want to start practising for our honeymoon.'

Coming Next Month

919 WAKING UP Amanda Carpenter
The boy next door is now the man with the golden future, while hers is still in question. What could they possibly have in common now?

920 A HIGH PRICE TO PAY Sara Craven
At the price of her mother's peace of mind and her sister's future, how can a young woman refuse to marry the one man who could give her family back everything her father lost?

921 A WORLD APART Emma Darcy
It's one thing to match wits with a fellow author on TV, quite another to be madly pursued by him in real life, where their values seem worlds apart.

922 ONE DREAM ONLY Claudia Jameson
The devastatingly attractive owner of a London toy company becomes personally interested in his new assistant. But she's afraid to risk involvement again—especially not his kind.

923 THE WADE DYNASTY Carole Mortimer
Sure, he proposed, but all he really cared about was control of the family's Alberta ranch. Still, with a family crisis reuniting them, can she deny her love for him a second time?

924 THE COUNTERFEIT SECRETARY Susan Napier
A widow tires of leading a double life—cool, efficient secretary at work, warmhearted mother of twins at home. But it's safer than falling in love with her boss, a self-proclaimed bachelor.

925 BEST LAID PLANS Rosemary Schneider
The right choice for a woman wanting marriage and children is a well-bred Boston banker, not the man with whom she shared a brief holiday romance. But love can disrupt even the best laid plans.

926 THE KISSING GAME Sally Wentworth
The new physiotherapist for a famous English soccer team expects some resistance to her appointment, but not from the youngest member of the board of directors. What could he have against her?

Available in October wherever paperback books are sold, or through Harlequin Reader Service:

In the U.S.
P.O. Box 1397
Buffalo, N.Y.
14240-1397

In Canada
P.O. Box 2800, Postal Station A
5170 Yonge Street
Willowdale, Ontario M2N 6J3

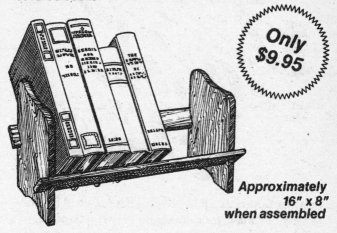

Where passion and destiny meet . . .
there is love

Jesse's Lady

Veronica Sattler

Brianna Deveraux had a feisty spirit matched by that of only one man, Jesse Randall. In North Carolina, 1792, they dared to forge a love as vibrant and alive as life in their bold new land.

Available at your favorite bookstore in SEPTEMBER, or reserve your copy for August shipping. Send your name, address, zip or postal code with a check or money order for $5.25 (includes 75¢ for postage and handling) payable to Worldwide Library Reader Service to:

Could she find love as a mail-order bride?

MARIANNE WILLMAN

PIECES OF SKY

In the Arizona of 1873, Nora O'Shea is caught between life with a contemptuous, arrogant husband and her desperate love for Roger LeBeau, half-breed Comanche Indian scout and secret freedom fighter.
